Reindeer Roundup
by

Kathi Daley

I want to thank the very talented Jessica Fischer for the cover art.

I so appreciate Bruce Curran, who is always ready and willing to answer my cyber questions, and Peggy Hyndman, for helping sleuth out those pesky typos.

A special thank you to Vivian Shane, Darla Taylor, Marie Rice, and Pam Curran for submitting recipes.

And, of course, thanks to the readers and bloggers in my life, who make doing what I do possible.

Thank you to Randy Ladenheim-Gil for the editing.

And finally I want to thank my sister Christy for always lending an ear and my husband Ken for allowing me time to write by taking care of everything else.

Books by Kathi Daley

Come for the murder, stay for the romance

Zoe Donovan Cozy Mystery:

Halloween Hijinks
The Trouble With Turkeys
Christmas Crazy
Cupid's Curse
Big Bunny Bump-off
Beach Blanket Barbie
Maui Madness
Derby Divas
Haunted Hamlet
Turkeys, Tuxes, and Tabbies
Christmas Cozy
Alaskan Alliance
Matrimony Meltdown
Soul Surrender
Heavenly Honeymoon
Hopscotch Homicide
Ghostly Graveyard
Santa Sleuth
Shamrock Shenanigans
Kitten Kaboodle
Costume Catastrophe
Candy Cane Caper
Holiday Hangover
Easter Escapade
Camp Carter
Trick or Treason
Reindeer Roundup

Zimmerman Academy The New Normal
Ashton Falls Cozy Cookbook

Tj Jensen Paradise Lake Mysteries by Henery Press:

Pumpkins in Paradise
Snowmen in Paradise
Bikinis in Paradise
Christmas in Paradise
Puppies in Paradise
Halloween in Paradise
Treasure in Paradise
Fireworks in Paradise
Beaches in Paradise – *June 2018*

Whales and Tails Cozy Mystery:

Romeow and Juliet
The Mad Catter
Grimm's Furry Tail
Much Ado About Felines
Legend of Tabby Hollow
Cat of Christmas Past
A Tale of Two Tabbies
The Great Catsby
Count Catula
The Cat of Christmas Present
A Winter's Tail
The Taming of the Tabby
Frankencat
The Cat of Christmas Future
The Cat of New Orleans – *February 2018*

Seacliff High Mystery:

The Secret
The Curse
The Relic
The Conspiracy
The Grudge
The Shadow
The Haunting

Sand and Sea Hawaiian Mystery:

Murder at Dolphin Bay
Murder at Sunrise Beach
Murder at the Witching Hour
Murder at Christmas
Murder at Turtle Cove
Murder at Water's Edge
Murder at Midnight

Writers' Retreat Southern Mystery:

First Case
Second Look
Third Strike
Fourth Victim
Fifth Night – *January 2018*

Rescue Alaska Mystery:

Finding Justice

A Tess and Tilly Mystery:

The Christmas Letter

Road to Christmas Romance:
Road to Christmas Past

Chapter 1

Friday, December 15

I wasn't sure exactly when the fog had rolled in, but I was having the darnedest time trying to figure out where I was and what it was I was supposed to be doing. Even though the fog was so thick I couldn't clearly define the images surrounding me, I could see red and green blinking lights overhead. I closed my eyes as nausea gripped me. I tried to focus and figure out what was going on, but the sound of "Rudolph the Red-Nosed Reindeer" blaring through loudspeakers was so jolting it caused my head to pulsate in time to the music. I had pretty much convinced myself I was trapped in some sort of Christmas nightmare when I heard the voice of my best friend, Ellie Denton.

"Zoe, are you okay?"

I tried to focus on her voice, but it seemed so far away.

"Come on, sweetie. Wake up. The ambulance is on the way."

Ambulance? Maybe I really *was* trapped in a nightmare.

"I think she's coming to," Ellie assured someone as the fog began to lift. I realized I was lying on my back on a hard object. Maybe the floor. I didn't have a clear sense of where I was or how I'd come to be there, but I could feel Ellie's hands stroking my hair as I made my way through the murky landscape toward the voice that was pleading with me to open my eyes.

"She's opening her eyes," Ellie screeched.

I cringed. My head felt like I'd partied way too hard and Ellie's happy chirps of relief weren't helping.

"Are you okay?" Ellie's brown eyes looked directly into my blue ones. "Do you feel any pain?"

"I'm fine. What happened?"

"You tripped over the elf with the candy canes and fell face first into Santa's lap. You have a huge bump on your head, but I think the baby is okay."

Baby? I reached down and touched my swollen stomach. Oh God, Catherine. "Are you sure Catherine's okay?" I croaked, barely able to find my voice.

"I think so. You tripped and fell to your knees. When you fell forward your face hit Santa's chair, but he caught you by the shoulders. You didn't hit your stomach. There's an ambulance on the way. Just lie still until it gets here."

As it turned out, lying still was all I felt up to, so I happily complied. I could hear people moving around, but it seemed like too much of an effort to open my eyes, so I simply allowed myself to drift into the space that exists between sleep and wakefulness.

As I waited for whatever would come next, I let my mind wander wherever it chose in an attempt to block out the chaos around me.

I'd been Christmas shopping with Ellie and baby Eli. We'd been marveling at the lavish holiday decorations the department store had set out this year when Ellie noticed a Santa sitting in a big red chair listening to the wishes of the boys and girls who'd been waiting in line. Ellie wanted to get a photo of Eli with Santa, so we'd headed in that direction. I remembered being a little sad that Catherine wasn't with us this Christmas, while at the same time being excited about what the new year would bring. I remember being worried, but for the life of me I couldn't remember why. I do remember the fear in my heart had caused me to become distracted, which is probably how I tripped over the elf in the first place.

"The ambulance is here," someone said.

I could hear rustling and shuffling but decided it still wasn't worth the effort to open my eyes, so I just lay there and waited.

"The ambulance is going to take you to the hospital," Ellie said. "I can't go with you because I have Eli with me, but I called Levi and he's on his way. We'll meet you there."

"Zak?"

Ellie took my hand in hers. "Zak isn't here, sweetie. Remember the accident?"

I cringed as my eyes closed tighter. Suddenly, I remembered what it was I'd been distracted by.

******

I wasn't sure how long I'd been asleep, but when I next opened my eyes Ellie was sitting in the chair next to the bed I was lying in. I was hooked up to so many monitors I couldn't begin to figure out what they were measuring, but I felt a lot better, so I hoped everything was fine.

"Ellie?"

Ellie set down the book she'd been reading and smiled. "Oh good, you're awake."

"Is Catherine okay?"

"Catherine's fine. You are as well. The doctor said you have a mild concussion and he wants to keep an eye on you overnight, but you should be fine to go home tomorrow."

I put my hand on my stomach and was greeted with a strong kick. There was no doubt in my mind that my daughter was going to be a soccer player. "What about the kids?"

"Levi picked Alex and Scooter up at school and took them home. Alex's working on the Santa's sleigh project and Scooter is finishing up a project for school. Levi, Eli, the dogs, and I are going to stay at your place for a few days. We don't want you to be alone while Zak's away."

"Does he know?"

Ellie shook her head. "I wanted to talk to you first. On one hand, Zak's your husband and should be informed of your little accident, but on the other, I felt like he already had a lot on his plate and didn't want to send him totally over the edge."

"I'm glad you waited to tell him. If you told him he'd only worry, and he really needs to focus on his mom right now. I'm fine, and with you and Levi to help me, I'm sure everything here in Ashton Falls will be back to normal in no time."

"Whatever you think is best. The doctor is on his way in to speak to you, so I'm going to go call Levi to let everyone back at the house know you're awake."

"Okay. And thanks, Ellie."

The doctor came in to do an exam as soon as Ellie left. I lay quietly, trying not to worry about my husband and the internal struggle we'd both been dealing with since we'd learned of his mother's accident. Any way you diced it, it was my fault Zak's mother was lying in a hospital in Paris, France, with serious injuries. No, I hadn't been driving the automobile that had run her down, but the only reason she was in Paris and not here, safe in Ashton Falls, was because she'd wanted to spend Christmas with us, I hadn't wanted her to, and Zak had wanted to make me happy. He knew reasoning with his mother wouldn't work, so he'd sent her to Paris for Christmas as some sort of a bribe.

Had there ever been a worse daughter-in-law than me?

"Are you feeling any pain?" the doctor asked.

"No. I'm fine."

"Your whole body just tensed up."

I let out a breath. "Sorry. I was just thinking about my mother-in-law. She was in a serious accident overseas and I guess I'm worried."

The doctor took off his gloves and took a step back. "That's understandable, but it's important that you try to relax. Your baby has been through enough stress for one day."

"I know. I'll try harder. Is everything okay?"

"Everything should be fine. I want to keep you overnight for observation, but you should be able to go home tomorrow. Your friend told me she'd be there to help you until your husband returned."

"She will. I'll have a lot of help."

"Okay, then. Get some rest and I'll check in on you in the morning."

I noticed my cell phone on the nightstand next to the bed. I picked it up and checked for messages. Although it was after six, I realized I hadn't checked my phone since before Ellie had picked me up for lunch and shopping. There were eight texts and two voice messages, but nothing from Zak. I figured he should have landed in France by now and would have called, but I supposed he had more important things on his mind.

The first text message was from my mom, asking me if I had any news on Zak's mom. I texted her back, letting her know I hadn't heard anything, but I'd let her know as soon as I did. I considered telling her about my own elf accident, but I knew she'd just worry, so I decided to wait until I was safely home before mentioning anything about it.

The next text message was from a woman named Stella Green. I'd gone to high school with her, but we hadn't stayed in touch, so I didn't consider her to be a close friend. The text just said *Call me*, so I skipped it and went on to the next.

The third text was from the Christmas store in town, letting me know the custom ornaments I'd ordered had come in and I could pick them up at my earliest convenience. I was excited to see how they'd turned out, so maybe I'd ask Ellie to pick them up for me.

The fourth text was from Stella again, asking me to call her and adding the words *it's really important* to the end. I once again skipped over it, figuring I'd call her after I got home.

The fifth text was from Scooter, asking if his friend Tucker could spend the night. I realized he'd texted before he knew I was in the hospital, but I decided to text back anyway, letting him know I was doing fine but he'd need to take a rain check.

The sixth text was from my grandfather's girlfriend, Hazel Hampton, asking if I was planning to participate in the cookie exchange this year. Knowing Ellie, she'd already made cookies for us both to bring, so I texted back to let her know I planned to attend and wanted to confirm the exchange was still scheduled for Tuesday.

The seventh text was from my mom again, asking if I wanted her to make a Christmas stocking for Catherine. I texted back that Catherine wasn't due until three weeks after Christmas, but if she had time and wanted to do it, we could always use the stocking next year.

The last text was from Alex, asking if I was okay. I guess Levi must have told her what was going on. I told her I was fine, but they wanted to keep an eye on me, so I was staying the night. I told her I'd call her later.

Both voice messages were from Stella. The first said she'd been getting strange emails and she wondered if Zak could help her track down the source. The second message sounded a bit tenser, as she asked me to please get back to her right away. I was about to call her when Ellie came in.

"So, everything went well?" Ellie asked.

"Yes. I can go home tomorrow. You don't have to stay with me. Go home to your husband and baby. I'll be fine."

"I know you'll be fine, but I'm not leaving until they kick me out." Ellie noticed the phone in my hand. "He didn't call?"

I shook my head. "He must hate me."

Ellie sat down on the side of my bed and took my hand in hers. "Zak doesn't hate you. He loves you. It's not your fault his mother was in an accident."

"If I hadn't been such a big, complaining baby she'd be safe and sound in Ashton Falls, making me crazy and not clinging to her life halfway around the world."

"You might not have wanted her to come to Ashton Falls for Christmas, but you didn't force her to go to Paris, and you certainly didn't force her to walk down a narrow street late at night where a drunk driver ran into her. Why was she walking down a narrow street late at night anyway?"

"I don't know. Zak doesn't know. It is rather odd."

"To be honest, Zak's mother doesn't seem the sort to walk anywhere."

"She's not. The whole thing makes no sense. Hopefully, she'll regain consciousness and tell us what happened."

Ellie squeezed my hand. "She will. She may already have. Chances are, Zak hasn't even made it to the hospital yet. I'm sure he'll call you when he has news to share."

I wanted to respond that I was sure he would, but I really wasn't so sure. I couldn't get out of my mind the haunted look on his face when he'd first received the call from the hospital in Paris. He'd looked so lost and scared. I wasn't used to my big, strong husband looking like a terrified little boy. I closed my eyes, fighting back my own tears.

"Are you okay? Should I call the nurse?"

"I'm just tired, and I can't help but worry about Zak and his mom. Let's talk about something else. Did Levi have a chance to talk to the guy who's running the new tree lot in town?"

"He tried, but the guy's being completely unreasonable. Despite the fact that his lot is right next door to the one Levi's running for the high school sports program, he maintains it's his right to sell his trees for whatever price he wants even though it's killing the high school's business."

"What I don't understand is how he's selling the trees so cheaply."

"It seems like he's using the cheap trees to get people onto the lot and then he sells them baked goods, ornaments, photos with Santa, and a variety of other add-ons for an exorbitant price. Levi's getting pretty frustrated, and I hear he's not the only one who's complained about the loud music and flashing lights, but it appears he has permits for everything, so there isn't a lot Levi can do."

"Poor Levi. It's really going to hurt the high school if they can't sell their trees."

"Yeah." Ellie sighed. "It really is. But I don't want you to worry about that or anything else. The doctor said you need to relax."

"It's kinda hard to relax with so much going on."

Ellie put her hand over mine. "I know, sweetie. But you need to try. If not for yourself, for Catherine."

Ellie was right. The past twenty-four hours had been so hectic, and I knew I needed to create a safe and stress-free environment for Catherine, so I tried to focus on happy thoughts. "The ornaments I ordered are ready at the holiday store. I don't suppose you'd mind picking them up on your way home?"

"I'd be happy to. And I love the idea of a custom ornament for each member of your family. I wish I'd thought of it, but it's probably too late to order them now."

"I was going to surprise you, but I ordered ornaments for you, Levi, Eli, and even Shep and Karloff."

Ellie's face softened. "Sweetie, that's so nice. Thank you so much."

"In addition to the ornaments I ordered for your family and mine, I also got ornaments for my parents and Harper," I said, referring to my sister, "as well as my grandpa and Hazel."

"I'm sure everyone will love them. It means a lot that you remembered us."

"I figured I'm not good at cooking or baking like you are and I can't sew like Mom can, but I can shop with the best of them and I wanted to do something special this year."

"Well, I'm excited to see what you got."

"Speaking of cooking and baking, Hazel texted me about the cookie exchange on Tuesday. I'm assuming you've made or will make cookies for both of us?"

"I'm totally on it. And we can go together, so you don't need to drive."

"Thanks, El. You're a good friend."

"I'm just trying to be as good a friend as my best friend."

I frowned. "You do mean me?"

"Of course, silly. By the way, the kids and I plan to finish decorating tomorrow, if it's okay with you. I don't want to intrude on your space, but I figured you probably wouldn't feel up to hanging the garland from the staircase or finishing the Santa's Village Zak was working on for the front lawn before he left."

"You're right. I probably won't be able to do it myself, but it would be nice to have everything done before Zak gets back. Alex knows where the garland for the stairs is stored and Zak had everything for the Santa's Village in his shed. Oh, and tell Levi not to forget to feed the reindeer. I know Zak went over everything with him before he left."

Zak had rented eight reindeer for the Hometown Christmas event that would be held from five p.m. on December 22 until five p.m. on December 24. The reindeer were in a pen on our property for the time being, but the events committee planned to truck them to a pen near the Santa's Village, which was currently being erected for the annual event.

"I'll make sure Levi feeds them using the notes Zak left. I don't want you to worry about anything. Levi and I will take care of everything."

"Thanks, Ellie. I feel like I should be home taking care of things, not lying here doing nothing."

"The kids will be fine. The house will be fine."

"I know. It's just such a busy time at the Zimmerman household. Tell Alex the check Zak left for her shopping trip with the Santa's sleigh committee this weekend is in the top drawer of Zak's desk. I think they plan to go to the mall in Bryton

Lake tomorrow to pick up whatever wish lists items weren't donated."

"I'll tell her. And don't worry. I have the impression Alex and her team have the whole thing handled."

"I'm sure they do."

"You look tired."

"I guess I am."

"Then I'm going to go and let you get some sleep. I'll be back in the morning."

"Okay. And thanks again."

As I closed my eyes in an attempt to fall asleep, I tried to focus on all the good things in my life. My wonderful husband and three honorary children. Pi was Zak's ward, or at least he had been before he turned eighteen. Currently, he was more of an assistant and would work full time for Zak once he finished college. He planned to come home for Christmas once he finished his last final on Wednesday. Scooter was thirteen and had first come to us when Zak agreed to babysitting duty after his mother died. Eventually, Scooter had come to live with us as well, and on a magical Christmas three years ago he'd brought with him his best friend, Alex, who had captured my heart the way no other child ever had. Alex was a brilliant and mature thirteen-year-old with a heart as big as creation. Last year she'd founded the Santa's sleigh program, collecting toys and food for those in need and then distributed wrapped gifts and food baskets a few days before Christmas.

And then, of course, there were the four-legged members of the Donovan-Zimmerman household. My dog Charlie, Zak's dog Bella, Scooter's dog Digger, and my cats, Marlow and Spade. Alex seemed to have a revolving door of animals she fostered, but right now all the animals that had been in her care had found forever homes.

And last but not least, I was blessed with the best friends in the entire world, Levi and Ellie. They'd been my friends for most of my life and I considered them family. As I drifted off to sleep, my thoughts changed to baby Catherine, who would soon make her entrance into the world. I didn't say so to Ellie, but even though Catherine wasn't due until after the first of the year, I'd gone ahead and bought an ornament for her just in case she decided to make an early appearance. I'd been having a few contractions in the past week and the doctor has assured me Catherine was fully developed, so if she did decide to arrive a couple of weeks early everything should be fine. It was strange, because one part of me was anxious for her arrival and another was terrified.

Chapter 2

Monday, December 18

It had been several days since my elf incident and I was mostly back on a normal routine. Ellie and family were still staying at the house and vowing to do so until Zak returned. I'd spoken to Zak, who'd assured me that his mom was doing better and out of danger, although she had several broken bones, so it would be a while before she was up on her feet. Zak thought she might be released later in the week, at which time he planned to bring her to stay with us until she had fully recovered. My guilt about her being in Paris in the first place was so acute I agreed with a level of enthusiasm I was far from feeling.

Still, she was Zak's mom and, of course, as her daughter-in-law, I was more than happy to do whatever it took to make sure she was happy and comfortable. I just hoped doing so wouldn't make me unhappy and uncomfortable. I wasn't sure exactly what I'd imagined my final month of pregnancy would be like, but so far, the reality hadn't come close to the intimate family-and-couple time I'd hoped for.

I'd been lying around for the entire weekend, so today I planned to go into town, check on things at Zoe's Zoo, the wild and domestic animal rescue and rehabilitation clinic I owned and my good friend Jeremy Fisher ran, maybe do some shopping, take in some lunch, and possibly even buy the items I needed for an album I wanted to make for all the photos I planned to take of Catherine's first year.

Before I could do any of that, however, I needed to make sure the animals were fed and settled. Levi had three more days of school before winter break, so he was at work, and Ellie had taken baby Eli to meet with her mothers' group for breakfast, as they did most Monday mornings. Alex and Scooter were at school, so it was just me for the remainder of the morning. I was about to head out to check on the reindeer when Jeremy called.

"What's up?" I asked.

"Oh good, you picked up. I've been trying to call you for the past hour."

"Why? What happened?"

"I'm afraid we have a reindeer situation on our hands."

"A reindeer situation?"

"Have you checked the pen at your house this morning?"

"No. I haven't been outside at all." I could feel panic begin to build as I tried to imagine why Jeremy had called. "I went along with Levi when he fed the reindeer last night and was heading out to check on them when you called. Is there a problem?"

"So far this morning, I've received reindeer sightings from one end of Ashton Falls to the other, including the passing lane on the highway, aisle eight at the supermarket, the Christmas tree display in the town square, and the gazebo in the park at the edge of town. The only reindeer I know of in the area right now are yours."

I took a deep breath, then let it out. "Hang on. I'm going to put on a jacket and check them right now."

I pulled on the old boots I kept in the mudroom, then slipped into my jacket. I went out the back door and toward the pen Zak had built for our visitors only to find it empty. I cringed when I realized I must not have latched the gate properly. I'd gone with Levi to see to the feeding. He'd gone into the pen while I'd waited safely near the gate. After he'd fed the animals he'd exited the pen and I'd latched the gate. Based on the fact that the gate was now standing wide open, I must not have closed it properly after all. If Zak didn't hate me for almost killing his mother, he was definitely going to hate me for losing his reindeer."

"As you suspected, they're gone," I said into the phone. "We have to get them back."

"I'm in the truck looking for them right now and Tiffany is on her way in. I spoke to Tank and Gunnar and they're willing to do an extra shift as well. We'll find them." Tank and Gunnar were the brothers who normally covered the overnight shift and Tiffany was the only full-time Zoo employee other than Jeremy.

"Zak's going to kill me."

"We'll round them up and he'll never even know they escaped. I'm going to swing by your house. Maybe we can follow the tracks in the snow."

"Okay. I'll call the local radio station and ask them to run a public service announcement warning people that reindeer can be dangerous and shouldn't be approached."

By the time I got off the phone Jeremy had pulled up. The problem with following the tracks in the snow was that there were so many going in every direction that there was no way to make heads or tails of them. Jeremy got a call about another sighting while we were looking around. After making me promise to leave the roundup to him, he headed toward town, where the sightings had occurred. I decided waiting at home when I really wanted to be helping Jeremy was going to make me nuts, so I drove into town as well to take care of at least a few of my errands. I meant to go to the craft store first, but the bakery seemed to be calling my name, so I made a sharp turn and headed in that direction instead.

"Can I help you?" a woman I didn't recognize asked.

"I'll have two sugar cookies and a bottled water. Where's Vivian today?"

"Her niece passed away. She's taking some personal time to be with her family."

Niece? Suddenly my heart sank to my feet. "Do you mean Stella?"

"Yes. She was found dead in her home yesterday morning. It's such a tragedy when we lose the young ones. That'll be four dollars and twelve cents."

"You're talking about Stella Green?"

"Yes, I'm afraid I am."

I handed the woman a five, told her to keep the change, grabbed my order, and headed toward the sheriff's office. The woman who manned the reception desk was on the phone when I entered the building, so I just waved at her and went down the hallway. Salinger, who was sitting at his computer when I walked in, looked up and frowned. "I was hoping because you weren't in here banging down my door first thing this morning that I was going to catch a break and you were going to stay out of things until after the baby was born."

"I was dealing with a reindeer emergency this morning, so I didn't hear about Stella until just a few minutes ago. What happened?"

"I assumed the reindeer escaped from the pen at your house."

"They did, but that's not why I'm here. Jeremy is out rounding up the reindeer. I'm here to talk about Stella. How did she die?"

"She was found by a neighbor in her apartment. It appears she died from blunt force trauma to the head."

"Stella left several messages on my phone on Friday regarding strange emails she'd received. I had my own head trauma to worry about, so I never did get back to her. We went to high school together, though we hadn't stayed in contact. It sounds like the emails could be a clue to who killed her. We need to get her computer to see what we can find."

"I agree, but I promised your long-suffering husband I'd do my best to keep you well away from anything dangerous during your pregnancy. Considering it appears you've lost his reindeer, I figure keeping you out of danger is the least I can do."

"I didn't lose Zak's reindeer. We know where they are. Sort of. Jeremy has been receiving calls about sightings; we just need to follow the tips, track them down, and return them to the pen. Jeremy said he'd handle it and I have faith he will. As for finding Stella's killer, I know Zak made you promise you'd do your best to keep me out of danger, and trust me, danger isn't what I'm looking for. I can't see my feet when I walk and I keep bumping into things in my own home. I'd be pretty helpless if I had to outrun a bad guy. But Stella reached out to me and I forgot to call her back. Now she's dead. I can't help but feel responsible. I need to be involved with this one. From the sidelines, of course."

"If Stella called you about strange emails it does seem that would be a good place to start, but I'm not sure how much success we'll have tracing the emails with Zak out of town."

I leaned back in the chair and rubbed my belly. "We don't have Zak, but we do have Alex. When it comes to hacking into places one ought not to be she's almost as good as her honorary father. She'll be home at three. Meet me at the house and bring the computer." I stood up, arching my back as I did. "In the meantime, I'm going to talk to a few people to see if I can get a better feel for what's been going on with Stella."

"You do know the meaning of the word *sideline*?"

"I do, but we need to find Stella's killer, and those closest to her are going to be more willing to speak to me than you."

"Maybe, but I still don't like it."

I shrugged. "Okay. Come with me. In fact, you can drive. People who are as pregnant as me shouldn't be allowed to drive anyway. By the time I push the seat far enough back so my stomach doesn't hit the steering wheel, my feet can barely touch the pedals."

"I assume you drove here?"

"I did."

Salinger held out his hand. "Keys."

"How will I get home?"

"I'll drop you off after we do our interviews."

"Very well." I handed Salinger the keys. "But we take my car to the interviews and you wait in the car. Some of Stella's friends have interesting pasts and aren't likely to tell me what they know if there's a cop lurking around."

"Okay. We'll do it your way for now. But you aren't to go anywhere out of eyesight at any time during these interviews."

We got into my car and I slipped a Santa hat that was on the backseat onto Salinger's head. "You'll look less conspicuous."

"Driving around with Santa is less conspicuous?"

"Stella has lived a colorful life and many of her friends hate cops. I think they're probably fine with Santa. Now remember, you drive and do the guard dog thing and I'll do the talking."

I decided our first stop should be Lucky's, a dive bar on the outskirts of town where I knew Stella liked to hang out from time to time. Salinger wanted to go in with me, but I knew that even wearing the Santa hat he'd be recognized. I persuaded him to wait in the car by agreeing to an open cell phone line so he could listen in.

It was early in the day. Other than the bartender and two men at the bar watching television the place was quiet.

"Whiskey?" the bartender asked.

"No, thanks. I just need some information."

"Don't talk to folks who aren't drinking."

"Okay, I'll have water. In a clean glass," I specified.

He poured me a glass of tap water and set it in front of me. "That'll be twenty bucks."

"Twenty bucks for water?"

"The water is free. The conversation is gonna cost you a twenty-dollar buy in."

I wanted to argue, but I also wanted out of the smoky room, so I gave him the twenty bucks. "You know Stella Green?"

"Yup."

"I guess you heard she's dead."

"Nope."

"Well, she is. I'm a friend of hers." He raised a brow. "Sort of," I clarified. "Anyway, I wondered if you could tell me the last time you saw her and who she might have been hanging out with then."

"Need a refill on that water?"

"No. I haven't even drunk what you gave me yet."

"It's twenty bucks either way."

I rolled my eyes. What a racket. I handed him another bill and he leaned in close, as if to disclose a secret.

"Stella got laid off from her job a while back and she fell in with a bad crowd. She was in a pretty low place, drinking every day and not stumbling home until I closed. Then a friend of hers hooked her up with a new job and she seemed to be getting her life back on track. I thought she was going to make a go of it, but then she started coming in again during the late hours. I asked her about it and she said she couldn't sleep and wanted some company. She lost a lot of weight and looked like hell."

"When was the last time you saw her?" I asked.

The bartender paused before answering. "I guess it must have been Friday night. She was sitting here at the bar and we were chatting. Her phone dinged and she stopped to look at it. She must have received a text. She finished her drink, got up, and left."

"You said she recently got a new job. Do you know where she worked?"

"The holiday store down by the park. She started when the store geared up for Halloween and then continued as Santa's elf. It was temp work, but she mentioned the owner really liked her and planned to keep her on after this season ended."

It seemed elves were becoming something of a theme with me; first I ended up in the hospital after tripping over one, then the woman I would have been helping if I hadn't been laid up had worked as an elf during the last days of her life. I chatted with the bartender for a few more minutes, but he didn't seem to know anything specific, so I decided to leave before the smoke got to me.

"You heard?" I asked Salinger after sliding into the passenger side of my car.

"I heard."

I glanced at my watch. "We should have time to stop by the holiday store before Alex gets home. Let's talk to Stella's boss. Maybe she'll have some insight into what was going on in her life."

As could be predicted given the fact that it was just a week until Christmas, the holiday store was packed. I had no reason to believe Mrs. Partridge, the store's current owner, wouldn't be comfortable speaking with Sheriff Salinger, so we both went in. Salinger must have forgotten he was still wearing the Santa hat because he didn't take if off before getting out of the car, and I didn't say anything because he looked so darn adorable.

"How can I help you?" Mrs. Partridge asked after Salinger asked to speak to her in her office.

"We're investigating the death of Stella Green," Salinger began. "I understand she worked here."

"That's correct," Mrs. Partridge answered. "She was referred to me by the son of my bookkeeper and was hired originally to help with the Halloween crowd but stayed on as an elf. She passed out candy canes and wrapped packages. Stella was doing an excellent job and I planned to hire her as a full-time employee after the first of the year. I was devastated to hear she'd been found dead in her apartment."

"I spoke to a friend of hers who told me she'd seemed scared and distracted the past few weeks," I said.

Mrs. Partridge frowned. "I'm afraid that's true. She was able to maintain a cheerful façade while at work, but I could see the fatigue in her eyes. I asked if she was having any problems in her personal life, but she told me she was fine. One of the other elves, a young woman named Connie, did say Stella had joined an online dating site. Connie seemed to think part of the reason she looked so tired was because she was going out a lot at night, but I sensed it was something more."

"The bartender at Lucky's told me that Stella frequented the bar quite often before she started working here. After that she seemed to become a lot more focused and appeared to be turning her life around, though he said she'd started coming in again in the past couple of weeks."

"That fits my impression of what was going on as well and would explain her fatigue. If you want to know more about her private life you might want to speak to Connie. She didn't confide in me."

"Is Connie here?" Salinger asked.

"Yes; I'll send her in."

Connie was a petite woman in her early twenties who made an adorable elf. Her teeny, tiny figure made me feel like a whale, which for some reason wasn't sitting well with me, but I plastered on a smile and listened intently while Salinger conducted the interview. It turned out Stella *had* joined a dating website and had been on quite a few dates with several different men over the past couple of months. She seemed to be having a good time and had met some really fun guys, but then she started receiving the emails and everything fell apart.

"Did she share with you what was in the emails?" I asked.

"No. She just said she felt like she was being stalked but didn't have any way to prove it. I think she was going to try to get hold of a friend she hoped could trace where the emails were coming from."

I groaned when I realized the friend she planned to contact was me. I'd really let Stella down, and while I couldn't undo what had been done, I intended to find out who'd killed her.

Chapter 3

We left the holiday store and headed toward Casa Zimmerman. When we arrived at the house, Alex was sitting in the kitchen chatting with Ellie while she fed Eli. As I knew she would be, she was thrilled to be allowed to help Salinger and me. She hooked Stella's computer up to Zak's system and began to keyboard, and I knew from experience all we could do was wait.

"I'm in," Alex said after a few minutes. "What do you want me to look at first?"

"Her emails," I said. "Her message to me was that she was receiving disturbing emails and hoped Zak could trace them."

I settled my bulky frame on a nearby chair while Alex typed. Zak was very gifted at what he did, but I could tell that with her intelligence and Zak's tutelage, one day she was going to achieve things we could only begin to imagine.

"She had passcodes on her email accounts," Alex informed me. "I should be able to get in, but it will take some time."

"Do you see anything about a dating site?" I asked.

"She has a link to Sexy Singles. It looks as though she's already signed up."

"Can you find her dating history?" Salinger asked.

Alex spent a couple of minutes navigating the site before she answered. "It seems she went on seven dates in the past eight weeks. The last one was two weeks ago with a man named Richard G."

"Is there a photo?" I asked.

Alex sent a photo of him, as well as his bio, to the large screen hanging on the wall. He was gorgeous, not at all like the type of man you'd think would need to use online dating sites.

"Can you print off a list of all the men she dated?" Salinger asked.

"Yeah, no problem." Alex hit Print. A single sheet of paper glided out of the printer and she handed it to Salinger.

"Tom S, Andy V, Ron P, Steve D, Eric M, Derek R, and Richard G. Do we have last names or contact information for any of these men?"

Alex took a couple more minutes to look around before answering. "Their profiles only show their first name and last initial. While the profile has a photo and a general description of their likes and dislikes, there isn't any personal information such as an email address, last name, phone number, or work location. If Stella met with these men I have to assume personal information was shared at some point. I can keep looking. I'll also keep working on the emails."

Salinger looked at his watch. "I have a meeting to get to. I'm going to have one of my deputies swing by to pick me up. Call me if you get into the email accounts."

"Will do," I promised before walking Salinger to the door.

"Do you really think you can get into the emails?" I asked Alex after Salinger left.

"Yeah, I think I can. If I get stuck I'll called Pi."

I had to smile as I watched Alex work. Her face demonstrated complete concentration, quite an admirable trait in a girl so young. "Can I bring you anything?"

"No, I'm fine. I'm hungry, though, and Ellie's making spaghetti, so call me when dinner's ready. I may be done by then, but if not, I'll take a break. I don't want to miss out on Ellie's meat sauce."

I supposed with Zak being gone it was a treat for the kids to have Ellie here. Zak did most of the cooking when he was home because I was slightly handicapped in the kitchen. In fact, given my condition, I was fairly certain if Ellie hadn't moved in with her family we'd be having pizza delivery or canned soup for dinner tonight.

Scooter was doing his homework and didn't seem to need any help, so I took Charlie and the other dogs currently in residence out for a short walk. Zak didn't want me walking on the icy beach trail—he was afraid I'd slip and fall—so he'd built a covered walkway with heat coils in the cement around the perimeter of the property. The dogs were able to run and play and I was able to keep an eye on them without the threat of ice. It was an extravagant addition, but Zak could afford it and he knew it would be important for me to get outdoors with the dogs despite my advanced pregnancy.

I felt a tinge of guilt as we passed the empty reindeer pen. I should call Jeremy to see how he was doing with them. I'd never forgive myself if one of the animals was hurt due to my carelessness.

"Hey, Jeremy, it's Zoe," I said when he answered my cell.

"Hey, Zoe. I was just going to call you. We've managed to capture Donner and Blitzen." The reindeer all wore harnesses with their names stamped on them in large, bright red letters so you could tell who was who. "I'm on my way to your place to return them to their pen."

"That's wonderful. And the others?"

"Dasher has been spotted on several occasions but, as his name would indicate, he's quick off the starting line and has managed to scamper away whenever anyone has tried to get near him. Dancer was last seen running down Main Street trailing a string of Christmas lights, and Prancer seems to be making his way along the river, which hasn't frozen over yet. Vixen, Comet, and Cupid haven't been spotted. It's those three who've disappeared who have me the most worried."

"I hope they're all okay. I feel terrible for not making sure the gate was secured. Not only is Zak going to kill me, I'll never forgive myself if something happens to one of them."

"You're being too hard on yourself. Mistakes happen. I don't want you to worry about this. I'm going to track them down and bring them home. All of them."

"How can I not worry? Several of them have been seen on the street. What if one of them is hit by a car?"

"Then we'll deal. Tiffany, Tank, and Gunnar are going to come in early tomorrow and we're going to find those we weren't able to track down today. I promised Zak I'd take care of everything while he was gone so you wouldn't need to worry and I'm going to."

"It sounds like Zak was running around town asking pretty much everyone to keep an eye on me. Salinger said Zak made him promise to keep me out of danger and now I find out he made you promise to make sure I didn't worry about things."

"He loves you. He wants your final month of pregnancy to go smoothly. So do I. So don't worry."

I sighed. "Easier said than done."

"I'll be at your house in five minutes. We'll get the two I have tucked in. Maybe the others will wander home on their own."

"Doubtful, but I guess we can hope. I'll take the dogs in and then wait for you out by the pen. Just pull around."

By the time Jeremy arrived and we'd transferred the two reindeer he'd caught to the pen it was dark. Jeremy fed the deer and I returned to the house. I took off my boots and jacket and headed in through the kitchen. Ellie's spaghetti sauce really did smell good. I'd gotten damp during my walk, so I went upstairs to change. On my way back down I poked my head in to check on Alex.

"I have something," Alex said.

"That was fast."

"It wasn't too hard to figure out her passcodes. She used her birthday, which I pulled from her Facebook page, for her personal email and 1, 2, 3, 4 for her dating site email."

"So she just had the two emails?"

"That's all I found. One looked as if she only used it to communicate with the men she found on the dating site, and she used the other for everything else. The emails sent to her regular account don't look suspect to me, but several of the emails on the dating site seemed pretty creepy."

"Creepy how?"

"I'm going to print them out, but basically they're all short and say things like 'I know where you live' and 'you can ignore me, but you can't hide.'"

I felt a chill run up my spine. That did sound bad. "Can you tell who sent the emails?"

"The emails were sent by DMG. All caps. They could be initials, a business, or even a dummy account. The email looks as if they were routed through the server at the dating website, the same as the others, but none of the men Stella dated had the initials DMG. The only one with a first name beginning with a *D* is Derek, but his last name begins with an *R*."

"Okay, I'll call Salinger to let him know. You did a good job. I'm proud of you."

Alex grinned. "Thanks. I want to look for a few more minutes before I quit for the day."

"Okay, I'll call you when dinner's ready."

I headed into the kitchen and took a seat at the table. There had been five emails from DMG. The first was sent two weeks ago. It was fairly harmless, letting Stella know he'd seen her profile photo and was interested in setting up a date. Stella had replied that she was uninterested in dating anyone else at that point. The next email from DMG was five days later, saying he knew Stella had dated a lot of men in the past month and he was just as much of a good-time guy as the men she had already gone out with. He strongly encouraged her to reconsider and go out with him. Stella didn't reply to that email at all. A few days later, DMG sent her another email scolding her for ignoring him. He said something about her "giving it away to everyone else," and he intended to "get in on the action." She ignored this email too. Then, at twelve noon on the last day anyone saw her alive, DMG sent the email about knowing where she lived and warning her not to ignore him if she didn't want to get hurt. Again, Stella didn't reply. The final email from DMG came through at 4:40 on the same day, telling Stella he would be by her place to pick her up at seven o'clock and she'd better be ready to give him what she'd given the others.

My heart pounded as I read the emails. Poor Stella. She must have been terrified. I wondered why she hadn't gone to the police. I'd never forgive myself for not helping her when she reached out to me, but there was one thing for certain: I would find the man who'd killed her.

The emails unnerved me, leaving me feeling exposed and vulnerable. I wished Zak was home and wanted to call him to see how things were going, but I figured it must be the middle of the night in France. I knew he was trying to arrange to get his mother home, but I hadn't talked to him all day and felt the need to connect even if just for a few minutes. I didn't want to wake him, so I chose to text him to let him know I was thinking of him. I figured he'd see the text when he woke up and know I loved and missed him.

When my phone rang less than a minute later I nearly dropped it. "Zak?"

"I saw your text."

"I'm sorry. I didn't mean to wake you. You usually keep your text messages on silent."

"I was awake. I'm glad you texted. I miss you."

"I miss you too. How's you mom doing?"

"Better. She has some healing to do, but she's out of danger. I'm trying to work out a way to get her home that won't cause her any more discomfort than she's already experiencing, but any way you slice it, a flight across the ocean would be hard on her. I spoke to Clara Fletcher and she offered to have Mom stay at her villa in Italy. I think I'm going to take her up on it." Clara was one of my mother's wealthy friends, and she'd helped us out on more than one occasion.

"Does your mom want to go to Clara's?" I asked.

"She'd prefer to come home with me, but I think she realizes it would be a tough flight. Mom met Clara at our wedding and seemed to remember her, so she's agreed to the plan. Clara's already at the villa for the holidays, so I'm going to arrange a flight for Mom on Thursday. I'll hire a nurse to care for her for the first week or two. I'll be home as soon as I get her settled in. Hopefully by the weekend."

The weekend seemed so far away, but I guessed I should be grateful that Zak's mom was going to be okay.

"That sounds like a good plan. Tell your mom I'm thinking about her and hope she gets better soon."

"I will. How are the kids?" Zak asked.

"Good. They miss you, but Levi and Ellie are staying here at the house until you get back, so they're being well fed and entertained."

"Is everything okay?" Zak asked with concern in his voice.

It may have been a tactical error to mention that Levi and Ellie were staying at the house.

"Everything's fine." I decided not to mention any of the things that were actually wrong, like Stella's death and the missing reindeer. "Ellie thought I looked tired, and you know what a mother hen she is."

Zak laughed. "I do, and I'm glad they're there. I hate being away from home so late in the pregnancy."

"I'm fine. Catherine's fine. We'll be waiting when you get home."

I could hear Zak yawn on the other end of the line. "You should get some sleep," I suggested. "Call me tomorrow if you have a chance."

"I will. I love you."

"I love you too." I couldn't quite prevent the tear that escaped from the corner of my eye as I hung up. God, I missed him.

Pulling myself together, I headed downstairs. Alex was in the kitchen helping Ellie get the food on the table. Ellie's meat sauce looked delicious. I sat down and tried to rub away the pain that had been building in my lower back.

"The last month is hard," Ellie said with sympathy.

"Yeah. I'm ready for Catherine to be here. I feel like an invalid most of the time. I can't even see my feet anymore."

"It won't be long now." Ellie bent down and gave me a hug. "Have you heard from Zak?"

"I just spoke to him. His mom is going to stay with Clara at her villa in Italy. Zak is going too, to get her settled, and then hopefully he'll be home this weekend."

"That sounds like a perfect solution. I was worried the flight home would be too much for her. And Clara's so sweet and funny. I'm sure Mrs. Zimmerman will enjoy her stay there."

"I hope so. I feel like everything is so out of kilter all of a sudden. I'll be glad when things get back to normal. Although I suppose with a baby on the way, I'll need to redefine what I mean by normal. Was it hard for you to get your bearings when Eli was born?"

"It was. I had this new person in my life who was very sweet but very demanding. We were in the middle of the remodel on the boathouse, Levi and I had just gotten married, and everything felt fragile. Things are better now. Things will get better for you too once you find a rhythm that works."

"I hope so," I repeated.

"I saw Jeremy pull up with the large-animal van. Did he find the reindeer?"

"Two of them," I answered. "He seems confident he can track down the other six. I feel terrible for not making sure the gate was latched correctly."

"You don't think someone intentionally let them out, do you?"

I frowned. "Who would do that?"

"I don't know, but it doesn't really track that you wouldn't secure the gate properly. You own a rehabilitation center that deals with wild animals like bears and cougars. You know how important it is to securely close gates. I've known you for most of your life, and while you're sometimes prone to missteps, I've never seen you be careless when it comes to the animals entrusted to your care."

I paused to think about that. "You may have a point. I remember latching the gate and then pulling on it to make sure it was closed. Maybe someone did let them out."

"You might want to add a lock to the gate just to be sure," Ellie suggested. "A bike lock would work."

"I'm sure there are extra locks in the garage."

"Ask Levi to see to it. It's better to be safe than sorry."

I went to the den, where I could hear Levi chatting with Scooter. I took a moment to smile at the scene before me. Eli was sitting in Levi's lap "helping" him work the handheld controller as he played a video game with Scooter. Eli was laughing and I hated to interrupt them, but I also didn't want someone letting the reindeer out again.

"Looks like a close game," I said as I entered the room.

"Eli's pretty good," Scooter said. "High-five."

Scooter raised his hand and Eli giggled as he high-fived him. It warmed my heart to know Catherine was going to have such an awesome big brother.

"Ellie thinks someone may have intentionally let the reindeer out. I think she may have a point. I want to add a lock just to be sure and I have one in the garage, if you can help me with it."

Levi set Eli on the floor in front of him and stood up. "No problem." Levi glanced at Scooter. "Will you keep an eye on him until I get back?"

Scooter looked so proud as he agreed to do just that.

I followed Levi into the garage and helped him find the lock. Then he went out to install it while I returned to the kitchen. "That's one great guy you have," I said to Ellie.

"Yeah, he really is great. There was a time I thought he'd make a terrible husband and father, but he's changed so much since Eli came into the picture. Where is Eli anyway?"

"Scooter's playing with him in the den."

"Dinner's almost ready if you want to let the kids know. Scooter can just bring Eli to the table. I'll put him in his high chair with some snacks."

I let Scooter know he should bring Eli into the kitchen and then wash up himself, and then I went to the computer room to tell Alex dinner was almost ready. Alex was on her cell phone when I entered the room, so I waited. Based on what I heard from her end of the conversation, it sounded like she was talking to someone about Santa's sleigh.

"Problems?" I asked after she hung up.

"Not really. One of the moms who was going to drive on delivery day has a conflict, but I'm sure I can find a replacement."

"When are you going to do the deliveries?"

"Saturday. I have some people coming by tomorrow evening to help me wrap everything. I hope that's okay. Ellie told me you had the cookie exchange, so I figured we wouldn't be in your way."

"That's fine. And I'm happy to help if you need an extra hand. I don't think I'm up to helping with the deliveries this year, but I can still wrap with the best of them."

"Zak told me not to let you tire yourself out. He wants you to rest."

"I'm fine. Really. And I want to help. Did you manage to get everything you still needed on your shopping trip this weekend?"

Alex nodded. 'I think so. Our list is even bigger than last year, but more people are aware of our project as well, so we had a lot more donations. Just don't go into the spare bedroom next to mine. There's so much stuff in there even I can barely walk around."

Alex turned back to the computer to log off just as a cramp squeezed my abdomen. I placed my hand on my stomach and gave it a gentle rub until the pain passed.

"Are you okay?" Alex asked, concern evident in her voice.

"I'm fine. Just a twinge."

"A twinge?"

"Sort of like prelabor contractions. They're pretty small and not all that painful. The doctor said they're perfectly normal during the final weeks of pregnancy."

Alex took my hand and led me to the kitchen. I could tell by the expression on her face that I hadn't alleviated her concerns, but Alex was a worrier. I'd need to do a better job of not giving her anything to worry about.

I couldn't help but smile as she and I entered the kitchen. It had been a really stressful day, but I found myself beginning to relax once we gathered around the table. Levi had funny stories to share about his day at the tree lot and both kids had things to tell us about school. I was confident Jeremy would find the reindeer; between Salinger, Alex, and me, we'd find out the identity of the person who'd taken Stella's life; and I drew a certain amount of comfort from the fact that Zak would be home in time for Christmas.

Chapter 4

Tuesday, December 19

I found I had a new outlook on life by the time the sun rose the following morning. Zak had left me a text letting me know his mother was going to be released a day early, which I hoped meant he'd be home a day sooner as well. Salinger had a few things to follow up on and promised to call me later as long as I promised to stay put. I said I would because I knew that was what Zak would want, though staying home when everyone else was out doing something was highly overrated. At least I had Charlie and the other animals around to keep me company. Tuesdays were usually busy, but the woman who'd taken Willa's place as events committee chairperson had changed the meetings to Wednesdays. Ellie and the kids had left the place spotless and Levi had taken the dogs for a long walk, so all I had to do with the rest of my day was relax.

Relaxing, I decided, was for the birds.

I'd promised Salinger I would wait here at the house for him, but that didn't mean I couldn't check out the dating site Stella had joined from the comfort of my own home. I decided the best way to check out the guys she had dated was to create a fake profile and try to set up chats with the same men. Alex had left a list of the men Stella had dated on the table near the computer, so I logged onto my own computer and went to the Sexy Singles site.

Name? Hmm. I obviously couldn't use my real name; I'd need to come up with an alias. Marilyn seemed to be a sexy name. I typed in Marilyn M, identifying myself as a twenty-six-year-old former model living in Ashton Falls for the winter so she could ski while she prepared for a movie role. Too much? Maybe, but I was willing to bet the guys who frequented the site were looking for a good time, not happily ever after.

The next thing I had to do was post a profile photo. I'm petite with dark curly hair, but I decided to make Marilyn tall and blond. I logged onto the internet and found a photo that seemed to represent the right mix of sex kitten and girl next door. I posted it, then created an email address through the dating site. I typed in a few hobbies and other personal tidbits to make Marilyn seem real and waited. It took only five minutes before the first request for a chat arrived in my inbox. It couldn't hurt to check it out. I clicked on the link.

Ron P was a single man in his early forties who lived in Bryton Lake. His hobbies included skiing and parasailing and his profile photo was decent. According to the contact history on Stella's dating dashboard, Ron P had been the third man Stella had dated. They'd shared three chats, which I imagine they'd both used to screen the other, before they set up a date. After a few minutes of exchanging pleasantries, Ron asked if I'd like to move over to a private chat room. I agreed and he provided a link.

"Ewww," I said out loud when I entered the room to find photos of whips and chains and all kinds of things I didn't want to see. What was wrong with people? I wanted to tell Ron to take a hike, but if he was one of the men who'd dated Stella I needed to engage him in conversation before that. I took a minute to ask myself what I needed to know about him. A full name would be nice, his phone number, email, and perhaps an address so Salinger could interview the guy.

I typed: *I noticed you like to ski. I love to ski. The snow up on the mountain is awesome right now. Weekends can be crowded, but I work for a restaurant, so I have Tuesdays and Wednesdays off when it isn't too bad.*

Ron typed back: *I work for the county, so I have weekends off, but I don't mind the crowds.*

Works for the county. Hmm. That narrowed things down a bit but not enough. I typed: *I have a friend who works for the county in road maintenance and he works weekends. I imagine you must work in one of the offices.*

I'm a planner, he typed, *so it's a nine-to-five gig.*

Bingo. I doubted there could be more than one Ron P who lived in Bryton Lake and was a planner for the county. I'd give the info to Salinger and let him follow up.

Another message from Ron P: *So, do you like to party? I'm always looking for someone who's into some one-on-one action. Maybe we could take the next step and set up a date of the role-playing kind.*

I returned: *I'd like to get together with you, but there's someone at the door so I have to run. Nice meeting you.*

I cringed after I logged off the dating site. Maybe this hadn't been the best idea. It appeared Stella had been attracted to guys who were total perverts and I didn't think I could even fake playing the role of a dominatrix.

I heard a car in the drive, so I logged off the computer and headed to the front of the house. I watched as Salinger got out of his squad car and came up the walk.

"You must have news," I greeted him as I opened the door and escorted him inside.

He nodded. "I was going to call, but I figured it might be a good idea to make sure you'd stayed put as I asked."

"I'm not a child."

"I know, but you're impulsive and I want to make sure you and your baby are out of harm's way. If that means working with you on this case so you're less inclined to go off on your own that's what I'll do."

"I have coffee in the kitchen and Ellie baked sugar cookies yesterday."

"I love sugar cookies."

I led Salinger through the house to the kitchen, in the rear. I poured Salinger a cup of coffee and myself a glass of water, then set a plate of cookies on the table. "So what do we know?" I asked.

Salinger bit into a sugar cookie before answering. "I spoke to the woman who runs the dating site. She gave me an overview on how it works, which could be helpful in figuring things out. Basically, there are three stages to the eventual personal meetup. In stage one, a man or woman sends a request to the person they're interested in getting to know better. The person on the receiving end can accept or decline the request to take it to step two. If the request is accepted, step two is for the two individuals to enter a chat room. Depending on how that goes, they can request a physical meet or not. If they both request one personal information such as an email address and telephone number are provided by the dating site."

"Okay, so do we know Stella's history with all three stages?"

"Stella declined an invite to chat with twenty-three men right off the bat," Salinger reported.

"She just looked at their photo or bio and hit Decline based on what she saw?"

"Exactly. Stella accepted the initial invitation to chat with nine men with whom she never requested a meet. The woman said just because Stella didn't request a meet that didn't mean they hadn't worked something out on their own. As we know, Stella went on physical dates with seven men."

"Did you ask the woman about DMG?"

"I did. She said each member sets up a personal email account. The accounts are considered to be owned by the person who sets them up and aren't monitored. She wasn't willing to give me access to the account or even to verify that DMG was a member. I'd need a warrant, but we'll need more to get one."

"Aren't threatening emails enough to get a warrant?"

"Not in isolation. Don't worry; we'll find the guy. You need to keep in mind that more often than not, running a murder investigation is a marathon, not a sprint. All we can do is follow up with each lead and hope something pops up as being significant."

"I have one lead for you. Stella's third date, Ron P, lives in Bryton Lake and works for the county as a planner. I figure that's enough to track him down."

"It is, but how do you know this?"

"That isn't important. What's important is finding Stella's killer."

"We'll revisit the method you used to obtain that information at another time. I agree finding Stella's killer is the most important thing. In fact, I'm heading over to her apartment to interview her neighbors as soon as we're done. The deputies who showed up on Sunday talked to a few people, but a lot weren't home. I'm hoping someone who hasn't been interviewed yet saw something."

I stood up. "I'm coming with you."

"I think it best you stay home."

"I'm bored. If you won't let me come with you, I guess I'll have to go out sleuthing on my own." I probably wouldn't follow through if Salinger called my bluff—I didn't want to put Catherine in danger—but I hoped my threat would be enough to convince him to let me ride along.

"I could just lock you up in one of the cells at the jail."

"You wouldn't."

Salinger shrugged. "It's tempting, but I guess I wouldn't actually do it. You can come with me because I don't think allowing you to ride along will put you in any danger, but I'm the one making the calls and you're to do exactly as I say."

"Deal," I said as I hurried down the hall to grab my coat and snow boots.

It was a bright, sunny day and the roads and sidewalks were clear and dry, yet Salinger insisted I wait in the car to avoid the risk of a slip and fall when we arrived at the apartment building where Stella had lived. I wanted to argue, but waiting for him in the car was a lot better than sitting around at home so I agreed, slipped off my jacket, and settled in to bide my time.

Luckily for me, one of Stella's neighbors approached the squad car. I rolled down the window and greeted the man, who looked familiar, though I couldn't place him.

"Has the sheriff taken to arresting pregnant women?" he teased.

"No. I'm just doing a ride along."

"I figured as much. I recognized you as the chick with a reputation for working with Salinger when one of Ashton Falls' residents meets a violent end. I'm Christopher, by the way."

"Zoe. You look familiar. Do you work in the area?"

"I wait tables at a couple of different places in town."

"Did you know Stella well?" I asked, jumping to the point.

"We weren't close friends, but we chatted if we ran into each other coming or going. I was real sorry to hear about her death. She was a nice woman, despite her crazy mood swings."

I leaned closer. "Mood swings?"

"Stella seemed to have a lot of problems. When I first met her, she seemed normal, but then she lost her job and started drinking a lot. That seemed to make her both hyper and depressed, depending on whatever else was going on in her life. Then she got the job at the holiday store and things seemed to get better. She was happy and her moods leveled off. She even started dating again."

"Did she ever bring her date's home?" I wondered.

"Sure, on occasion. I don't think she dated any one guy for long, but it seemed she'd been dating frequently toward the end."

"Were you home this past weekend?"

"I was in and out. I work a swing shift at the Wharf, so I sleep late in the mornings. I was just waking up when the cops showed up on Sunday. One of Stella's coworkers stopped by to check on her when she didn't show up at work for the second time in as many days and found her dead."

"When was the last time you saw her?" I asked.

Christopher paused to consider my question. "I guess it was Friday. She was going out at the same time I was on my way to work."

"Did she say where she was going?" I asked.

"She said something about getting hammered. I had the feeling she'd had a bad day and needed to blow off some steam. Stella didn't say as much, but I think she was having guy problems."

"Why do you say that?"

"I saw her sitting in a car with a man when I came home from work on Thursday night. He was yelling at her and it looked like she was crying. It was dark, but the car was parked under a street lamp; while I couldn't get a good look at what was going on, I got enough of a glimpse to know Stella wasn't having a good time."

"Do you remember what time it was?"

"I guess around midnight. I got off at eleven and had stopped for a drink on the way home."

"Did you ask Stella what had been going on?"

He shook his head. "It was her business and I didn't want to get involved."

"What kind of a car was it?"

"Black Mustang. Newer model. I'd say not more than a couple of years old."

"Did you happen to notice a license plate number?"

"Nope. I wasn't paying that much attention. I noticed the car had something dangling from the rearview mirror. I'm not sure what."

That didn't narrow it down much, although with Ashton Falls' heavy annual snowfall, most people drove four-wheel drives, not sports cars. "Did you see what the guy looked like?"

"It was dark and I didn't get a good look. Seemed like he had dark hair. If I knew what was going to happen I would have paid more attention to the details, but as it was, I just walked by."

I glanced up to find Salinger coming in my direction. "Thanks for the input."

"No problem." He waved as he turned to leave. "I'll see you around."

Salinger slid into the driver's seat, then turned to look at me. "Who were you talking to?"

"His name's Christopher. I didn't catch a last name. He lives in the building."

Salinger frowned.

"Hey, you said stay in the car and I stayed in the car," I said, heading off any complaints. "He came over to me."

"Did he know anything?"

"He said he saw Stella arguing with a man in a black Mustang at around midnight on Thursday. He didn't get a license number, but he saw something hanging from the rearview mirror. He also saw Stella leaving her apartment on Friday afternoon. She told him she was going to get hammered. We know she went to Lucky's; we just don't know what happened after that."

"The neighbor who lives beneath Stella heard her arguing with a man on Friday night. She'd been asleep, so she wasn't sure what time it was, but she thought it must be late. She said it sounded like they were throwing things at each other. She considered calling the police to file a noise complaint, but then the arguing stopped and everything was quiet after that. The medical examiner puts time of death between midnight and four a.m. on Saturday morning. My guess is whoever Stella was arguing with is the person who killed her."

"Too bad the neighbor didn't follow her first instinct to call the police. Stella might be alive if she had."

"Perhaps."

"Did you find out anything else?" I asked.

"Most of Stella's neighbors were out. I did speak to one woman who said she ran into her a week or so ago. Stella was dressed up and appeared to be going out on a date. She introduced her to the man she was with and she seems to remember the man's name was David."

"I don't remember David as being one of the names from the dating site," I said.

"It wasn't. The last man she dated from the site was two weeks before her death. She must have met the man she was with that night some other way."

I paused and looked back toward the building. It was two stories, with eight units on each floor. There was a covered parking garage off to one side and a covered walkway connecting the apartments to the garage. The man I'd spoken to had said the Mustang had been parked under a street lamp, so the car must have been parked on the street in front of the building. I wondered why Christopher had been walking there in the first place. If he'd parked in the garage and then taken the walkway to his apartment he wouldn't have passed the Mustang at all. I supposed he might have gotten a ride home from work that night and been dropped on the sidewalk in front of the building.

"I'm sure you searched Stella's apartment for physical evidence, but as long as we're here, do you think we could take another look?"

"If I say no will you come back on your own?"

"Probably."

Salinger opened his door. "Put your coat back on. It's chilly out there."

The first thing I noticed when I entered Stella's apartment was a large bloodstain on the carpet. I wasn't normally squeamish, but Catherine might be; I had to put my hand over my mouth to avoid losing my breakfast. The apartment looked like it hadn't been cleaned in quite some time. Not only was there a sink full of empty wineglasses but there was a lamp on the floor and clothes lying on almost every piece of furniture. I bent down as much as my swollen belly would allow and looked under a chair. The colorful object I'd noticed there on further investigation turned out to be a Skittle. "You know what's odd?" I asked. "The apartment is a mess, but the floor looks like it was vacuumed recently. In fact, if I had to guess I'd say it was vacuumed after Stella fell to the floor."

"Why do you say that?" Salinger asked.

"There are clearly lanes created by the wheels and brush of the vacuum everywhere in the room except this one location." I pointed to the spot on the carpet, where the large bloodstain had been left after the body was moved. "It almost looks as if someone vacuumed around the body after she was dead, or at least after she was lying on the floor."

"Why would anyone do that?" Salinger asked.

"Maybe to hide evidence." I looked around the room. "Let's see if we can find the vacuum. Maybe whatever someone was trying to hide is still in the dust bag."

As it turned out, the bag that should have been hanging on the back of the unit was missing. It looked like the killer was smart enough not only to clean up any evidence but to take it with him.

"Did you find the murder weapon?" I asked.

"Negative. The ME determined Stella was hit with a pointed object. It could even have been the corner of something. It's possible the killer took the weapon with them."

"I guess there really isn't anything to find here. Thank you for humoring me."

"Happy to do it if it will keep you out of trouble. I need to head back to the office, and then I'm going to have a conversation with Ron P. I'll drop you back at your house on the way."

"Actually, drop me by the Zoo instead, please. I want to check on a few things there, and I'm sure Jeremy will give me a ride home."

Chapter 5

I couldn't help but smile when I walked into the Zoo. I loved this place, but circumstances dictated that I hadn't been able to spend as much time there as I would have liked. It was especially festive, with an artificial tree standing in the corner and red stockings with white brims hanging from the reception counter.

"I wasn't expecting you in today," Jeremy greeted when he joined me in the lobby, where I was looking through adoption forms.

I picked up one of the puppy ornaments we were giving away this year from the basket on the counter and hung it on the tree. So far, I hadn't participated in the decorating at all, so now I could say I had. "I wasn't planning to come in, but no one's at home and I was bored. How are we doing with the reindeer roundup?"

"I've spent a good part of the morning driving around looking for the tricky beasts, but they're a lot wilier than you'd think. Tank and Gunnar managed to round up two more this morning and are on their way to your place to drop them off. That means we're halfway there."

"If the deer took off into the woods they're going to be hard to track."

"It seems as if the deep snow has them sticking to the roads and the open areas in town. With any luck, we'll have the other four home by the end of the day."

"I hope so." I couldn't help but worry about the animals, who'd been bred and raised in captivity and weren't used to the dangers that could be found in the wild. "How's the bear cub that was brought in from the fire down south doing?"

"Better. I was worried about her at first, but she's healing nicely."

I paused to straighten a large red bow. "And the dog and cat adoption clinic?"

"Successful. I think we should find homes for most of the domestic animals by Christmas. If things go as planned I'm going to give Tiffany a few days off. Tank and Gunnar agreed to hold down the fort over Christmas, and if all they need to keep an eye on are the bears, it should be easy for them to handle things."

"Sounds workable. Are you still going down south to spend Christmas with Jessica's family?" I asked, referring to Jeremy's wife.

"We leave on the twenty-second," Jeremy confirmed. "Personally, I'd rather spend Christmas at home, but Jess is excited about the trip and I want to make her happy."

"I'm sure you'll have fun. It's important to be with family at Christmas."

"I guess. I try to avoid my family at all costs, but Jessica is a lot closer to hers."

I picked up a stack of mail. "I'm sure her family will go out of their way to make you feel welcome. If not, it's only for a few days. I'm going into my office to check on a few things. Can you run me home in an hour or so?"

"Yeah, no problem. You didn't bring your car?"

"Salinger dropped me off. He doesn't want me looking in to Stella's death on my own, so he's letting me tag along with him."

"Does he have any leads?"

"Nothing concrete, but I'm working on a few ideas too. You don't happen to know anyone in town who drives a black Mustang, do you?"

"Cory Wood bought a Mustang a year or so ago. Why?"

"Stella was seen arguing with a man in a black Mustang the night before she died. Does Cory still work at the auto repair shop?"

"As far as I know. You don't think Cory killed Stella?"

I shrugged. "Probably not. But if he was with her on Thursday night he might have some idea why she ended up dead on Friday night."

"If you're going to talk to him I'm going with you. We'll stop by the auto shop on the way to your place."

******

Vern's Auto Repair had been around since before I was born, located in an old building I was certain was held together with grease from all the cars that had been worked on over the years. Vern was an old-school mechanic who liked to work on the older model cars, but he'd hired several mechanics fresh out of school to take care of the newer-model vehicles that required a knowledge of the computers they were equipped with.

"Can I help you?" a man I didn't recognize asked.

"We're here to speak to Cory," Jeremy answered.

"He's on a break. Come back in thirty minutes, or you can look for him at the diner next door."

We decided to try the diner, where we found him sitting in a booth by himself. Jeremy greeted him and we slid into the booth across from him. The distance between the seat back and the table was tight, and I found I had to sit sideways to make room for Catherine.

"So, how can I help you?" Cory asked after taking a large bite of his M&M pancakes, which were piled high with whipped cream. Talk about sugar overload.

"Zoe's looking in to Stella Green's death. We heard you'd spoken to her recently and hoped you might have some insight into what was going on in her life," Jeremy began.

Cory squinted his eyes, as if he were trying to make up his mind about me. "I know you aren't a cop. Were you a friend of Stella's?"

"We went to high school together, but we hadn't stayed in touch. She left me several phone messages on the day she died. I never got back to her and I feel bad about that and want to try to help find her killer."

Cody leaned forward. "What exactly is it you want to know?"

"I spoke to one of Stella's neighbors who informed me that he saw you speaking to her on Thursday night."

"Yeah; so?"

"The neighbor said it appeared as if you were arguing."

Cory took a deep breath. "Is that what this is all about? Someone saw me arguing with Stella and now you think I killed her?"

"Did you?" I asked.

"Of course not. I worked late on Thursday, trying to fix a transmission that was determined to stay broken. I was tired and frustrated, so I stopped off at Lucky's for a pint before I went home. Stella was there and I sat down next to her, but as soon as we started talking I realized she was hammered. I didn't want her driving home in that condition, so I carried her out to my car and drove her to her apartment. Of course she was royally pissed. She kept insisting she was fine and wasn't ready to go home, but I'd seen her go down that path before, so I wasn't buying it. By the time we got to her building I'd had enough and let her have it. Verbally, not physically. Other than carry her to my car, I never touched her."

"Did she say anything that might explain why she ended up dead and who might have killed her?" I asked.

Cory rubbed his jaw. "She did keep going on about some guy hassling her, in the context of trying to convince me that she had a good reason for getting drunk. I figured it was just some lame excuse for doing what she wanted to do. I used to be good friends with her brother, so I've known her for quite a while. She went through a bad breakup a while back and sank into a really dark place. We ran into each other then, and I felt sorry for her, so I tried to help. I even helped get her a job at the place my mom works. I thought she was doing better; then I saw her at the bar and realized she was up to her old tricks."

"So your mom must be the bookkeeper at the holiday store," I said.

"Yeah, so?"

"The owner of the store just told me the son of her bookkeeper was responsible for getting Stella her job there. Did Stella give you any indication of the identity of the man who was hassling her?" I asked.

"She didn't say, but I know she was hanging out with a guy called Docker. I don't know his real name, but he works at Lucky's a couple of nights a week, which is where Stella met him."

"Do you know which nights he works there?" Jeremy asked.

"Usually Sundays and Mondays. He works at the ski resort as a lift operator the rest of the week."

"Okay; thanks," I said. "Before we go, is there anything else you can tell us?"

Cory shrugged. "Not really. I hope you catch the guy who did it. She could be dark and depressed at times, but then, sometimes she could light up a room with her smile."

We thanked him and returned to Jeremy's truck.

"So what now?" Jeremy asked. "Do I take you home or do you want to drive up to Eagle Mountain to see if Docker is working today?"

I hesitated. I knew Jeremy was busy, but I did want to speak to the man Cory had indicated had been spending time with Stella. Everyone would have a fit if I went alone, so I decided to have Jeremy make the drive up the mountain. It would be a fifteen-minute trip each way, plus the time it took us to track down and speak to Docker, but finding Stella's killer seemed to be the most important thing right then.

Jeremy called the Zoo and spoke to Tiffany, who had just returned from reindeer patrol. She'd recovered one of the reindeer who'd been seen walking down Main Street, so now they only needed to find Dasher, Comet, and Vixen. Jeremy promised to keep an eye out for tracks and to return to the Zoo as soon as we'd finished our errand.

We were halfway up the mountain when one of the reindeer ran across the road less than a hundred yards in front of us.

"Do you have the tranquilizer gun?" I asked.

"I have it. I'll get the reindeer; you call Tiffany and tell her to bring the van."

The idea was to tranquilize the reindeer and then use our large animal van to transport him back to the pen. My instinct was to follow Jeremy into the deep snow as he tracked the animal, but one look at my huge belly convinced me to wait in the truck as I'd been told.

Twenty minutes later, Tiffany showed up with the van, which was towing a trailer with a snowmobile and a sled. "Has Jeremy caught up with him yet?" Tiffany asked.

"The last I heard, he was getting close, but not close enough to take the shot. The snow is pretty deep, so it's slow going."

Tiffany slid the sled from the trailer, then backed down the snowmobile. "I guess I'll just wait for Jeremy to radio us. If I show up with the snowmobile before the reindeer is all the way under it will probably scare him."

"It's chilly out here," I commented. "Let's wait in Jeremy's truck."

After we were settled inside, Tiffany turned on the ignition and cranked up the heater.

"If we can get this one tucked back into the pen we'll only have two more to track down," Tiffany commented as she rubbed her hands in front of the vent. "The fact that this one is so far up the mountain has me concerned, though. The farther they roam from ground zero, the harder it's going to be to find them."

"Yeah." I sighed as I looked out the window at the flurries that were just beginning to appear in the sky. "There does seem to be some urgency in getting everyone back where they belong."

"Did you have any luck with the guy who was seen talking to Stella?" Tiffany asked.

"He didn't seem to know a lot, but he did give us the name of someone who works at the resort, which is why we were on this road in the first place. By the time we get the reindeer settled into the pen it'll be too late to look for him today. I may just see if Ellie can drive me up there tomorrow after the events committee meeting. We've been talking about taking a drive to the village to look at the decorations anyway."

"Jeremy to Zoe, come in," Jeremy said over the radio. "He's down. Send Tiffany in with the sled."

"Ten-four," I answered. "Tiffany is on her way."

I was fortunate to have such talented, caring individuals at the Zoo. The work we did was important, and it meant a lot to me that those I depended on to care for the wild and domestic wildlife in the area cared about the animals they were tasked to rescue and skilled at what they did.

By the time I got home the sun had already set. Ellie was busy preparing dinner when I walked into the house and Scooter and Alex were sitting at the kitchen table decorating sugar cookies.

"More cookies?" I asked.

"I wanted to have cookies to serve at the wrapping party tonight, and Scooter and I are both taking some to school," Alex answered. "And Ellie thought you should have extra to take tonight for the cookie exchange."

"Did you round up enough help with the wrapping?"

"I have ten kids coming from school. I thought we'd set things up in the living room, if that's okay. Levi's going to bring in those long folding tables you have in the attic."

"Sounds like a good plan. Do you have enough supplies?"

Alex nodded. "We have everything we need. I think we're going to make a lot of families happy this year."

I smiled. "I think so too. I'll help you decorate the cookies after I wash up."

As I passed the living room on my way to the stairs, I stopped to watch Levi playing with Eli. Father and son were crawling around on the floor looking for a red ball that was sitting in plain sight, though Levi was pretending he couldn't find it. Eli was in front of the Christmas tree laughing and clapping his hands. I rubbed my stomach. Next Christmas it would be Zak playing with Catherine in front of the tree; the thought gave me a warm, happy feeling from the bottom of my feet to the top of my head.

******

Hazel had a beautiful home she took a lot of care to decorate each year. She liked to play hostess so, in addition to hosting the weekly book club I belonged to, she hosted the cookie exchange and several open houses and parties during the holiday season. My own home was decorated beautifully, but Hazel had a certain elegance and style neither Zak nor I possessed. My home was warm and cozy, while Hazel's was classic and sophisticated.

"Your house looks lovely," I said to her as I handed her the plate of cookies Ellie had made. "You've added some touches since I was here last week."

"Decorating seems to be one of those things you never really finish." Hazel set the plate on the table with the others. "Every time I think I'm done I have an idea for something better."

"Zak's the same way. He's like a kid in a candy store when it comes to holiday decorations."

"Have you heard from him? How's his mother?"

I poured myself a glass of nonalcoholic punch. "She's doing better, considering. She's staying with Clara Fletcher in Italy until she recovers enough to take the flight home."

"Clara's such a nice woman. I'm sure Zak's mother will get the rest she needs staying with her. It's too bad she won't be able to join you for Christmas, though."

"Yes," I said, despite the fact that it was my not wanting her to be here for Christmas that had caused the problem in the first place. "Although with everything that's going on, it's rather hectic at my place. I'm sure she'll be better off with Clara."

Hazel poured coffee into mugs with poinsettias on the side. "I spoke to Alex yesterday. It sounds like she's been busy with Santa's sleigh ride."

"She has, but she's very organized and seems to have everything under control. I feel bad I can't do more to help this year."

"I'm sure Alex understands you can't be running around town delivering gifts in your condition. I told her I'd take lead with one of the teams, and she has plenty of students lined up to help as well. It's too bad we couldn't work it out to have Zak's reindeer pull a real sleigh."

"That would have been fun, but with all the reindeer excitement we've already had this week, trying to harness them might have been pushing it."

"I heard about the great reindeer escape. Have you managed to round them all up?"

"Almost. Jeremy and the crew have done a fantastic job. I'm hoping they'll all be home by the end of the day tomorrow. I'll feel a lot better when I know they're all safe."

"Luke told me it's possible someone might have intentionally let them escape," Hazel said.

"Pappy's right; that might be the case. At first I thought I'd been careless with the latch, but the more I think about it, the more certain I am that I pulled on it to make sure it was secure before I walked away."

Hazel set the mugs of coffee on a tray with cream and sugar and placed it on the main snack table. "Who would do such a thing?"

"I don't know, but there's a lock on the gate now. The only people with the combination are Jeremy and my crew, Levi and Ellie, and Alex and Scooter in case of an emergency. Once I get all the reindeer home I want them to stay there—at least until they're scheduled to be transported into town for Hometown Christmas."

I followed Hazel back into the kitchen, where she picked up napkins. "I can't believe that's this weekend. December has flown by."

"It really has. I just hope everyone's ready. It's very odd trying to plan an event without Willa at the helm."

"Yes." Hazel sighed. "She's been missed. And not just in her role as committee chairperson. Willa was a good friend for a lot of years. I'm still not over the fact that she was taken from us."

Hazel and I both took a minute to remember our friend, who'd been murdered just a couple of months earlier, before we headed into the living room, where the others were waiting. I took a seat next to Ellie, suddenly feeling sad rather than joyful. Ellie smiled at me and squeezed my hand. Knowing Ellie, she'd seen Hazel and me talking and figured out the rest.

"You should talk to Phyllis about Stella," Ellie whispered.

Phyllis King was a dear friend and the administrator of Zimmerman Academy, the private school Zak ran.

"Phyllis knows something about Stella?" I asked.

"She spoke to her last week. Stella was coming off her shift at the holiday store and seemed depressed, so Phyllis offered to buy her dinner. She said she thought Stella was holding something back, but she did talk a bit about what was going on in her life."

I glanced at Phyllis, who was chatting with one of the women from book club. I knew once Hazel made the introduction to the exchange we'd play a few games. I'd head to the kitchen then and motion for Phyllis to join me.

When we were in the kitchen I asked Phyllis what she knew about Stella.

"I see Ellie told you that we had dinner last week. The poor girl seemed so lost. I wanted to help her, but I don't think I was able to make much of a difference in her life."

"Would you mind sharing what you talked about?"

"Let's have a seat." Phyllis and I sat down at the kitchen table. "I'd known Stella for quite a few years. Her mother and I were friends, and I used to visit their home when she was growing up. Stella was always such a moody child. She'd be happy and carefree one minute, then dark and depressed the next. I suggested to her mother that she might have a chemical imbalance that would respond to medication, but I'm not sure she ever followed up on it. But I digress. You asked me about my conversation with Stella last week, not the emotional disorder I believed she might have had as a child."

"I imagine both were important in understanding her behavior, but only the more recent event will help us identify her killer," I pointed out.

"Very true. When I spoke to Stella last week I wanted to find out why she was so down. It took a while for me to get her to open up, but eventually she said she'd joined a dating site and met and gone out with several men. She didn't seem happy about it and I made a joke about none of them being keepers. She responded that all the men she'd dated were one-night stands. Assuming one-night stand was the preference of the men, I made a comment about that, and she informed me that all she was after was one night of sex, that the decision not to pursue a second date with any of the men had been hers. I'll admit I was a bit shocked at her attitude. It wasn't my place to lecture her about her standards, so I changed the subject. Looking back, I sensed anger as I spoke to her, but I also sensed fear. I wish now that I hadn't let the fact that I was appalled by her behavior prevent me from continuing the conversation."

I sat quietly for a moment, trying to process what Phyllis had said. I knew Stella had made dates with seven men from the dating site. The fact that she'd only seen each man once seemed important; I just wasn't sure why yet. I'd planned to call Salinger in the morning to find out how his meeting with Ron P had gone. Maybe I'd contact a few others to see if I could engage them in a chat.

"Did Stella mention any of the men by name?" I eventually asked.

"No, not that I remember. As I said, I tuned out when she began to discuss the sexcapades."

"Thanks for sharing what you have. My Zodar is telling me the information is relevant. I'm not sure how yet, but I hope Salinger and I will be able to figure it out."

After my conversation with Phyllis I found I'd lost my enthusiasm for the cookie exchange. Ellie had given me a ride over and I hated to ask her to leave early, so I stayed in the kitchen to call Salinger. He didn't pick up, so I left a message and went back to the fun and games. I loved Christmas, but this year, with everything that was going on, I was having a hard time finding my Christmas spirit.

"Everything okay?" Ellie asked when I returned to my spot next to her on the sofa.

"I'm fine. A little tired, I guess."

"I'm tired as well. Let's make our excuses to Hazel and sneak out early. Warm jammies, a Christmas movie, and a crackling fire feel just about perfect."

"Actually, there are ten high school students at the house wrapping presents, but I guess we can sneak up to my bedroom and curl up with a good movie. I'm sure Scooter and Levi are in the den watching something with a lot of shooting and car chases."

"Hiding out in your suite sounds like a wonderful idea. I'll bring Eli in with us so I don't have to worry about him. If we sneak in through the back entrance the wrapping gang won't even know we're home."

Chapter 6

Wednesday, December 20

The new committee chairperson, who was also the new county clerk, was Hillary Spain, a nice enough woman, though, like Willa, she tended to be a stickler for the rules. The real problem, I'd come to discover, was that while Willa had enforced a certain structure, she was well acquainted with local and county ordinances and how they pertained to the projects the committee became involved with; Hillary seemed to be making stuff up as we went along. Ellie thought we should give her the benefit of the doubt; she was a young woman trying to get a foothold in the community. Ellie felt once she settled in she'd relax a bit and, in the end, turn out to be the strong chairperson we needed. I wasn't sure I agreed, but I hoped Ellie's faith wasn't misplaced. So far, the planning for this year's Hometown Christmas celebration, the event that kicked off in just two days, had been teeming with one problem after another. Luckily for me, due to my state of unwieldiness I hadn't been asked to participate on any level.

"All but two of the food vendors are confirmed," Ellie reported, "but the two who are holding out for kitchen space in the community center are the largest in terms of selection."

"If we let the food vendors use the community center we won't have anywhere for the kiddie carnival," Tawny Upton argued. "We tried doing an outdoor carnival in the past, but if the weather's bad no one will be willing to stand in line."

"Are those vendors asking to use the whole community center or just the kitchen?" my dad, Hank Donovan, asked.

"They'd like to use most of the indoor space," Ellie confirmed. "They made a good point about it being much too cold to eat outside."

"Have we had the food vendors indoors in the past?" Hillary asked.

"We've done it both ways," Ellie explained. "We've used the entire community center as a food court, with everything centralized, but we've also had the food vendors spread throughout town. There are advantages to both, but we're expecting snow, so I think an indoor area to eat is a must."

"What about the cafeteria at the elementary school?" Levi asked. "It's not too far off the beaten path and it won't interfere with the kiddie carnival. We could even offer rides between the community center and the school."

Ellie glanced at Levi. "I'm not sure the food vendors will go for that. I have a feeling they'll be concerned that the lack of convenience will reduce the number of customers they get. I know if I was walking around enjoying the festivities I'd probably just eat in one of the restaurants in town rather than getting onto a shuttle to have lunch."

"What about a tent?" Hazel suggested. "We could let the food vendors use the community center kitchen to prepare the food, then set up an eating area in the parking lot behind the building."

"That could work as long as we had heaters to keep the area warm," Ellie responded.

"It seems it makes more sense to put the kiddie carnival in the tent and let the food vendors have the whole community center," I said, speaking up for the first time. "Better yet, let's just have the kiddie carnival in the elementary school. Ellie made a good point about people not wanting to get on a shuttle to eat, but I'd be willing to bet the kids will make sure Mom and Dad get on the shuttle if that's the only way to play games."

"I agree with Zoe. The kiddie carnival should move to the elementary school," Dad said.

We discussed the situation a while longer and eventually agreed to house the larger food vendors in the community center, the carnival at the elementary school, and have the smaller snack and drink vendors spread out around town. After that we discussed the community play, the Victorian carolers, and the voting for the window displays. By the time the meeting was over I was starving. My mom was babysitting Eli, so Ellie and I had the whole day to ourselves. We decided to head up to the ski resort and have lunch there before tracking down Docker.

The resort provided a large village with lodging, restaurants, shopping, and even a small movie theater.

Like most destination areas, Eagle Mountain went all out with decorations that created a magical, snowy wonderland for ski enthusiasts who elected to spend the holidays on the slopes.

"I love coming up here at Christmas," Ellie commented as we wound our way up the mountain toward the village. The ski area had strung white lights in the trees that lined the road on both sides, creating a Christmassy feel before visitors even reached the village.

"I've been dying to hit the slopes," I admitted. "Of course the ski season is going to be half over before I'm able to enjoy all this powder. Zak bought us both season tickets, but I'm not sure I'll get my money's worth out of mine."

"Once you recover from the delivery I'll be more than happy to watch Catherine if you and Zak want to go skiing," Ellie volunteered. "I'm sure your mom will be willing to babysit as well."

"Mom's already trying to arrange an overnight stay for Catherine and she isn't even born yet. I thought she was going to be upset about being a grandma, but she seems almost as excited about the baby as Zak and me."

"Of course she's excited. We all are. By the way, as long as we're all the way up here, remind me to check out the new ski apparel. I think I might get Levi a ski jacket for Christmas. His old one is looking a bit worn."

The conversation stilled as Ellie and I took in the canopy of lights strung over the entrance to the parking lot. We parked and headed to the village, which was not only decorated with lights, real fir garlands, and bright red bows, but featured a skating rink in the center.

"Oh, look at the mechanical bears." Ellie grabbed my hand and pulled me toward an area that had been made up to look like an enchanted forest. "I'm going to have to bring Eli up here before Christmas. He'll love the moving bears and the cute little penguins chasing each other across the pond."

"It's pretty awesome, but I'm starving. There's that new pub I've been wanting to try. Not that I can drink, but I hear the food is delicious and the tables overlook the beginners' hill. It'll be fun to watch people learn how to ski while we eat."

"Sounds good to me," Ellie replied.

We'd just turned in the direction of the pub when the sound of screaming filled the air. I stood in stunned disbelief as one of the runaway reindeer ran down the middle of the courtyard, causing people to scramble to get out of his way. Ellie pulled me through the doorway of one of the shops.

"You'd better call Jeremy," Ellie said.

"I was just thinking the same thing."

I spoke to Jeremy, then Ellie and I grabbed sandwiches to go and waited for him and his reindeer tracking crew in the parking lot. It looked like Ellie and I would have to wait for another day to check out the pub, but as soon as Jeremy arrived to take over the campaign to capture our escapee, Ellie and I could set out to track down Docker.

******

He was working one of the lifts at the base lodge, which meant we wouldn't have to take a lift up the mountain to meet with him. As soon as I explained that I wanted to speak to him about Stella, he arranged to talk to us near the fire pit during his break. Covered but with open walls, the fire pit was quite warm if you could snare a seat on one of the sofas closest to the fire.

"Oh look, a sofa just opened up," Ellie said before elbowing her way through the crowd to grab it before anyone else did.

I waddled along at a much slower pace. After settling onto the sofa, we ordered hot cocoa to sip while we waited.

"I wonder how Jeremy's doing," Ellie said.

"I told him to text me with an update. If he's successful in capturing this reindeer we'll only have one more to find."

"It's kind of sad to interrupt their fun to return them to that small pen," Ellie observed.

"I agree, but they could get hurt or hurt someone while they're on the loose. It's a miracle none of them have been hit by a car. When they aren't on display they live on a ranch up north, so I doubt they've had much experience with vehicles speeding down the highway at sixty miles an hour."

The waitress had just brought our beverages when Docker arrived. I scooted closer to Ellie to make room for him, which created an intimate setting for a conversation as serious as the one I planned to have with him.

"Would you like something to drink?" I asked.

"No, thank you. I only have a short break. You said you had some questions about Stella?"

Even though Docker was sitting right next to me, I realized I was going to have to raise my voice to be heard over the loud Christmas music coming from the nearby skating rink.

"I guess you heard she was found dead in her apartment."

"Yes, I had."

"She'd reached out to me before her death, but I was in the hospital at the time and didn't get back to her in time. I feel terrible and want to find out who killed her. I spoke to Cory at the auto shop and he was the one who told me that you were friends. I hoped you could tell me what had been going on in her life."

Docker squinted and chewed his lip, and I suspected he was trying to decide whether to confide in me. He must have judged me harmless because he shifted slightly and turned to face me. "Stella went through a bad breakup a while back. She took it hard and ended up drinking a lot more than she should. She lost her job, which sent her even further over the edge. I work at Lucky's two nights a week and she was there every night I was for a while, so we'd talk. She had a lot of baggage to deal with, but Cory helped her get a new job and she finally realized she was over the loser who'd dumped her. It seemed her life was getting better."

"And then…?" I asked. So far Docker had told me the same things I'd heard from everyone else.

"And then Stella decided she wanted a new guy in her life, so she joined a dating site. I thought internet dating was a bad idea, but she assured me that she wasn't looking for a husband, just some companionship, and she didn't see how meeting men to have dinner with could hurt."

"And then…?" I repeated.

"And then someone started sending her weird emails. At first she thought the emails could be coming from one of the men she'd dated, but eventually, she decided they had to be from one of the men she'd rejected."

"You mean men she'd chatted with but decided not to meet?"

"Right."

"So Stella thought one of the men who belonged to the site she'd chosen not to date had become obsessed with her."

"That was her theory. I asked her why she was sure the emails weren't from one of the guys she'd gone out with, and she felt confident all the men she'd met were fine with one-night stands. She didn't think any of them would hassle her."

"Okay, that gives me something else to look at. I know Stella received a text or email while she was at Lucky's on Friday. She left shortly after and was dead by the next morning. Did you see her on Friday night?"

"No. I had a date with another lift operator. We were together from the time we got off work on Friday until we came here on Sunday morning. I can give you her phone number if you want to check it out."

"Thanks. I believe you, although Sherriff Salinger will probably want the information. Maybe you should give it to me and I'll pass it on to him. It'll save you both some time."

Docker jotted down the name and phone number and left to return to work. Ellie and I spent the rest of the afternoon looking through the colorfully decorated shops. As we were preparing to leave, I received two texts. One was from Jeremy, letting me know the reindeer we'd seen was safely tucked into the pen at home, leaving only one on the loose, and the other was from Salinger, saying he had a new lead he wanted to discuss with me. Ellie wanted to get home so she could pick up Eli; Levi was picking Alex and Scooter up from school. I asked her to drop me at Salinger's office. He could drive me home after we'd talked.

******

Salinger was waiting for me in his office when I arrived. The first thing I did was share my conversation with Docker, which made him frown. I assured him that Ellie had been with me the whole time and we'd been in a public place and so in absolutely no danger. I wasn't sure he bought that, but he took the information for Docker's alibi before he began to tell me why he'd called me.

He'd finally been able to speak with one of Stella's neighbors, who'd spoken to her about her experiences on the dating site. She'd told her Tom S was a ski instructor at the resort and Eric M worked for the refuse company. She didn't know anything about the other men, but once Salinger'd had jobs to match the first name and last initial he was able to track down both men.

"So, did you find out anything that might help us narrow things down?" I asked.

"Both men, as well as Ron P, who I spoke to yesterday, told me the same story. They'd contacted Stella through the dating service. She'd told them she was looking for a good time but nothing serious. All three men were fine with the arrangement. They all said they went out with Stella once, had a wonderful time, and never saw her again."

"That fits with what Phyllis told me. Stella told her she was looking for a single night of fun and nothing more. Did the men have alibis for Friday night?"

"Yes, they did. Tom S, whose last name is Silverman, told me that he happened to run into Stella a few days before she was murdered. She told him that she was going to quit the dating site because of some correspondence she'd been receiving."

"So we're back to the emails."

"It would seem so, although I still plan to find Steve D and Derek R."

"What about Richard G?"

"I tracked him down through his cell phone. Although Stella's cell hasn't been located, I was able to pull her phone records. She received a text at 10:42 on the night she died from a phone registered to Richard Greenly, who confirmed he was Richard G from the dating site. I asked him about the text and he said he'd been returning a message he had received from Stella earlier in the day regarding a book he'd recommended to her but she'd forgotten the name of."

"Do we believe his story?"

"I don't know," Salinger said. "It didn't appear he was lying, but the bartender said Stella got a text or email while she was at the bar and left. It's possible the ding the bartender heard was from an email, not a text. Greenly was a lot more guarded about his date with Stella than the others were. I'm not saying he killed her, but he remains on the suspect list for now."

"I'm not saying he's innocent, but a ding on a phone can be a lot of things. A text, an email, an instant message on Facebook, even a tweet or Instagram alert. I don't suppose a ding on a phone in isolation tells us much. Do we know what time Stella left the bar?"

Salinger sat back in his chair and steepled his fingers. "No, but I'll find out. Your explanation of the various reasons a phone might ding gives me an idea. Maybe it's time to look at Stella's social media accounts. It seems nowadays a lot of folks post the everyday details of their lives to one account or another. Maybe Stella did as well. It could be her accounts will tell us the identity of Steve D and Derek R. We might even get a handle on what she was doing during the last week of her life."

"Good idea. Alex still has Stella's computer. I'll have her look at it after dinner, which I should get home to. Can you give me a ride? Ellie just dropped me off here."

Salinger opened a drawer and took out his keys. "Okay, but no more sleuthing without my being in the loop. Even if you're with someone like Ellie or Levi. I know you think you're just talking to people, but remember, talking to people in the past has landed you in some pretty precarious situations."

"I know. And I don't want to put Catherine in danger. If I have a thought or idea I promise to call you before doing anything."

"Good. And call me after Alex has a look at the social media accounts. There could be something there, but if we come up cold I think I'm going to have another chat with the woman who runs the dating site. If Stella's stalker was one of the men on the site he might have stalked other women in the past."

Chapter 7

Thursday, December 21

I woke to snow falling outside my bedroom window. The kids were off school for winter break beginning today, so I didn't have a reason to rush out of bed. Charlie was lying near my legs, while Marlow and Spade were curled up on Zak's pillow. I pulled the heavy comforter up to my chin and settled in for another hour of sleep. I wasn't sure if it was the pregnancy or the stress that Zak's absence had caused, but I hadn't slept well all week and as each day had passed I'd found myself getting progressively more tired.

I was just nodding off when my phone rang. I considered ignoring it, but it could be important, so I rolled over and reached for the annoying device. I smiled after looking at the caller ID.

"Good morning," I greeted Zak.

"It's actually afternoon here. I should have considered the time difference. Did I wake you?"

"No, I was awake. It's snowing and the kids are on break, so Charlie and I decided to be lazy and lounge around under the covers for a while longer. I'm glad you called. Marlow and Spade have been filling the void of not having you in bed with me, but I think I'm ready for a return of the real thing."

Zak sighed. "Yeah. Me too. It's been a rough week."

I sat up and shifted the pillows behind me so I had a soft place to rest my back. "How's your mom?"

"Considering the extent of her injuries, pretty well. She was discharged this morning and we arrived at Clara's a little while ago. I've hired a nurse to live in until Mom's up and around. I didn't want Clara to have to feel like she needed to take care of her or be available twenty-four-seven. The nurse is a very nice woman close to Mom's age. I think they'll get along fine."

"I hope so. I really do feel bad about things."

"It's not your fault," Zak assured me. "Mom never should have been walking in that alley after dark."

"Did she happen to tell you why she was in the alley in the first place?"

"She can't remember. She remembers going to dinner with the friend who came on the trip with her and then nothing until she woke up in the hospital. I spoke to her friend and she said they'd had a spat during dinner, so she called a cab and left, while Mom elected to stay and finish her meal. She doesn't know what happened after that. The whole thing is very odd."

"Yeah," I agreed. "It really is. Maybe your mom will remember what happened after she has a chance to heal a bit."

Zak let out a breath. "Yeah, maybe. So, how's everyone doing?"

"Everyone's great. The kids are really looking forward to Christmas and we're all excited about Pi coming home. I know his last test was yesterday. Did he say when he'd be arriving?"

"He's flying in tomorrow. I arranged for him to rent a car, so no one will need to go pick him up. He's going to be home for three weeks; I figured he'd want his own wheels anyway."

"Yeah, that's a good idea. Do you know what time he'll be here?"

"I think his flight gets in at four. I told him to text you when he landed. How are things at home?"

"Things are good. Scooter told me that he got an A on the project he's been working on for school and Alex seems to be on top of everything regarding Santa's sleigh ride. Levi and Ellie finished decorating, so all you'll need to do when you get home is relax."

"And you haven't been overdoing?"

"I've been doing my best to let everyone wait on me." I decided not to mention Stella's death or the missing reindeer. Zak couldn't do anything to help, and if I told him what was going on he'd just worry.

"I'm happy to hear that. It's important that you take it easy and conserve your energy while you can. Listen, the nurse I hired just walked in and I want to go over a few things with her. I'll try to call you later."

"Okay. I love you."

"I love you too."

I was glad Zak had called, but he'd sounded so tired. I wished I'd been able to go to Paris with him, but with only weeks before my due date, there'd been no way. Hopefully, Zak's mom would enjoy spending time with Clara at the villa and Zak could relax and enjoy what was left of the holiday season. He'd assured me over and over again that nothing was my fault, but I couldn't quiet the little voice in my head that kept saying it really was, at least partially.

I was awake and the urge to stay in bed had passed, so I put my feet over the side of the bed, slipped on my robe and slippers, and headed to the bathroom. Before he'd left, Zak had decorated our suite. Not only was there an artificial tree in the corner near the fireplace, but he'd placed bright-red and green bows around the room. The brown rugs that usually covered the bathroom floor had been replaced with red ones, as had the towels that were hung near the sink and the tub. There was no way you could spend time in the room and not end up feeling very Christmassy.

The house was quiet when I arrived downstairs. I wasn't sure if everyone was still in bed or if they were up and gone. Deciding to enjoy the quiet, I made myself some breakfast, then settled at the kitchen table to eat it. I'd barely taken two bites when my phone rang again. This time it was the sheriff.

"Hey, Salinger. What's up?"

"I thought you were going to call me after Alex had a chance to look at Ms. Green's social media accounts."

"I was, but then it got late. I can talk now, though, if you have a minute."

"I'm all ears. What'd you find?"

"Stella had accounts in all the normal places, but it didn't look as if she'd written any new posts for more than a year. She'd been tagged by others a few times and several friends posted birthday greetings on her Facebook page back in August, but as far as updates or even shared pictures, we didn't see a thing. What we did find were a lot of check-ins. While Stella may not have shared news or photos, she tended to check in several times throughout the day. And not just when she was doing something fun or unique. There were check-in posts from regular places like the gas station and the post office."

"Did she check in the last day of her life?" Salinger asked.

"Four times. It looks like she must have had the day off. She checked in from Rosie's at one-thirteen p.m., Lucky's at six twenty-two, the truck stop out on the highway at ten-fifteen, and the liquor store on Fourth Street at eleven twenty-two."

"It sounds like it might be worth our while to talk to the clerks at the liquor store. You said you had texts and phone messages from Stella on the day she died. What time did those come through?"

"The first text, which just said, *Call me*, arrived at twelve-nineteen. The second text, which said, *Call me, it's important*, came through at one o'clock on the dot. The first phone message, in which she said she'd been getting strange emails and wanted Zak to help her, came through at two-ten, and the last phone message, which sounded tenser, arrived at four fifty-seven. She must have gone to the bar after that."

"Okay, that could help. Now that we know her movements for the day, maybe we can put together a time map. It sounds like something may have happened between the two phone calls. Perhaps she received another email, or even a phone call or text. I have the emails Alex printed out and the phone records. I'll see if I can pinpoint the reason behind the second, tenser voice message."

"Alex and I already mapped the emails. Stella received two emails from DMG on Friday, one at noon and the other at four-forty. Both were threatening, and the second one informed Stella that he was going to come by to pick her up at seven. She went to Lucky's at six twenty-two, probably to avoid DMG."

"Sounds like we really need to track down this DMG."

"Agreed. Do you have anything else to tell me?"

"The woman from the dating site had second thoughts and provided contact info for Derek R and Steve D. I'm on my way to talk to them now. How about I pick you up at one? I'll take you to lunch and we can brainstorm."

Okay, pause everything right there. Had Salinger just asked me to lunch? I frowned. We got along fine, but not once in all the years I'd known him had he asked me to lunch or any other meal for that matter. "Are you feeling sorry for me?" I asked.

Salinger chuckled. "I can't pull anything over on you. And yes, I guess I am feeling a bit sorry for you. You're not only very pregnant but your husband's halfway across the world, and I can sense your frustration at not being able to dig into this mystery the way you normally would. Besides, we both have to eat, so how about it?"

"Okay," I decided. "I'll be ready."

The fact that Salinger wasn't simply tolerating my presence in his life but was actually seeking it out was too weird for me to digest, but I *was* frustrated at not being able to do more and he'd opened a door, so who was I to refuse to enter?

I finished my breakfast, then went upstairs to shower and dress. When I came back down the house was still quiet. I didn't think it likely that everyone was sleeping in, which could only mean they were all out. I wondered where they'd gone and why they hadn't left a note. I texted Alex to see if she knew what was going on. Shortly after, she texted me back and said she was shopping with Ellie and Eli, and Levi had taken Scooter with him to the Christmas tree lot so they could bring the larger trees to the front to try to pull in more customers.

Which meant I was alone in the house until Salinger picked me up. It was still snowing, so taking a walk didn't make sense. And I realized I shouldn't be out driving around. Which left... what did that leave? I was used to being over-the-top busy and had no idea what to do with time on my hands.

After wiping down the already spotless kitchen counters and attempting to read a book, I logged on to the dating website to see if I'd had any new hits. I had no intention of ever sharing my real name with any of the men who contacted me, but I hoped if I chatted with a few of them as Marilyn, I'd pick up a clue as to how Stella's death and the dating site were related, if they were.

I gasped when I connected to the site: 142 emails? I narrowed my gaze, then went to my dashboard. Unless something was very wrong with the site's system, 142 men had indicated they'd like to chat with me since I'd last logged on. Perhaps I'd done too good a job of setting up my fake profile.

I didn't want to take the time to go through every email, so I hit Decline next to the profile photo of each man. The thing was, even if I accepted a few all I'd end up with was an eyeful of stuff I didn't want to see.

Logging off the computer, I decided to call my mother. I hadn't spoken with her for a while and we still needed to firm up our plans for Christmas. "Hey, Mom," I greeted her when she answered.

"Zoe? Is everything okay?"

"Everything's fine. I just thought I'd call to say hi."

There was a momentary pause on the other end of the line. "Are you sure you're okay?"

"I'm sure. Why would you think otherwise?"

"You never call me just to chat."

I supposed Mom had a point. I wasn't good about calling just to say hi, and we saw each other fairly often. "I just wanted to firm up our plans for Christmas. It's only a few days away."

I could almost feel Mom relax. "Of course. I guess we do need to get organized. Initially, we talked about having Christmas Eve at your place and Christmas dinner here. Are you still up for that? I can do both here if it would be easier for you."

"No, I still want to do Christmas Eve dinner. Zak should be home by Saturday and Ellie is here to help with the cooking. With Grandpa and Hazel, I guess we'll have thirteen."

"That sounds right. How's Zak's mom doing?"

"Zak's getting her settled at Clara's today. If all goes well, he'll try to come home tomorrow. It'll be late and he'll be exhausted by the time he gets here, but at least he'll be home."

"I'm sure he's as anxious to get home to you as you are to have him home."

I looked out the window at the Christmas wonderland Zak had set up in the yard earlier in the month. It looked extra pretty with the fresh snow on it. Too bad he wasn't here to enjoy it.

"Dad and I are taking Harper to look at the windows tonight. You should come with us. Bring the kids. Levi and Ellie are welcome too, if they'd like."

"I guess Christmas has sort of snuck up on me. I'd like to look at the windows. Hometown Christmas starts tomorrow, and the streets will be packed. It probably would be best to go tonight."

"Great. I'll make us a reservation for dinner as well."

"Sounds good. I'll text Ellie to make sure they want to go and then get back to you to let you know."

I hung up the house phone and picked up my cell. There was a message letting me know I had an email. I clicked over to the email account I'd set up through the dating site and found an email to Marilyn from a man who identified himself as *Interested*. He said he'd like to get to know me better and gave me the internet address of a chat room where he wanted to meet.

Okay, that was odd. How did he get my email address? It was supposed to be private until I authorized the dating site to share it with a potential date. I was going to delete the email but decided to wait and show it to Salinger.

******

Salinger frowned as he looked at the email. "You think this was sent by the same person who sent the emails to Stella?"

"I don't know. I could ask Alex to run a trace, but I don't want to scare her. There's a good possibility it was sent by someone else entirely."

"I thought you were going to stay on the sidelines with this one."

I flinched just a bit at the angry tone in Salinger's voice. "I *am* on the sidelines. I never even left my house. I just thought if I set up a dummy account I might be able to get a feeling for the type of man Stella was dating. I hoped I might even be able to strike up conversations with a few of them."

"You realize that if the man who killed Stella somehow hacked into her account at the dating site to get her email and then traced it back to an address, there could be a killer out there who knows where you live? Or at least where *Marilyn* lives."

"The hacker won't trace the email back to me. Stella didn't have the security system on her computer that Zak has installed on ours. If the person who sent the email tries to trace it back to a physical location he won't get far."

"I hope you're right, but I don't like this one bit. We need to trace not only this email but the ones sent to Stella. And we need to figure out who DMG is."

"I'll call Alex and tell her to meet us at the house. Don't worry, we'll figure it out."

"I hope so." Salinger shook his head, then leaned back in the booth. I could see he was stressed, and I was sorry to have been the cause of it, when I'd had only good intentions.

"I'm sorry. I really am. But maybe we should look at this as a positive. We managed to smoke out someone who could very well be the killer. Maybe if I respond he'll send another email. The more information we get, the better the chance of figuring out who murdered Stella."

I waited for Salinger to disagree, but he didn't. But he didn't agree either. All he did was sit across from me and glare, though at least he wasn't yelling or threatening to lock me in a jail cell.

"Look," I said after a minute of awkward silence, "I screwed up. I'm sorry. I want to help, but from this point forward I'll let you make all the calls. I'll be available for brainstorming, but other than that I'll stay out of it."

Salinger still didn't speak, but I could tell he was listening.

"The person who sent the email will never know Marilyn and I are the same person," I tried to reassure him. "I was careful. I not only used a fake name and profile photo but the hobbies and whatnot I posted are very general. There's nothing that in any way links Marilyn to me. It'll be okay."

Salinger sat forward and looked me in the eye. "So, you set up an email address through the dating site that you don't use for anything else?"

"Correct. It's registered to Marilyn M. I used a fake phone number and it didn't ask for a physical address."

"And you're sure the hacker who managed to retrieve the information can't trace it to the computer in your house?"

"I'm sure. No one is better at hacking than Zak, which means no one knows how to set up a security system better than he does. Our system is unhackable."

"I guess that makes me feel a little better. And you made a good point about using Marilyn to smoke out the person who sent the emails to Stella."

We stopped talking as the waitress delivered our lunch. We began to eat before resuming our conversation.

"Tell me everything that's happened since you set up the fake profile," Salinger said.

"Not a lot. I chatted with Ron P, which is how I found out where he worked. After I logged off I got busy and never logged back on. When I checked the site this morning I had over a hundred messages. I figured that was too many to weed through, so I declined them all. Shortly after that I received the email."

Salinger leaned his elbows on the table. "It sounds like we could be on to something with the idea that the person we're looking for may not be one of the seven men Stella dated but one she rejected right off the bat."

"That would be my take on things."

"Okay. Let's script a reply email to Interested and then head over to the liquor store Stella checked in at just hours before she died. Maybe she was with someone, and if we're lucky a clerk will remember who it was, or the store will have surveillance cameras."

I couldn't help but grin. I loved the fact that Salinger was treating me like a partner. I knew his motivation was to keep an eye on me and make sure I didn't get into any trouble while Zak was away, but I was enjoying the give and take the two of us were engaged in.

We decided we'd arrange for a face-to-face meeting with Interested. He'd show up and question the guy about the email and the fact that he seemed to have access to an email that should have been secure, while I waited safely out of the spotlight at home. We sent off the email and headed to the liquor store while we waited for a reply. With any luck, we'd have Stella's killer identified by the end of the day.

The liquor store where Stella had checked in the night she died was located on the outskirts of town. Salinger wanted me to wait in the car while he spoke to the clerk, which didn't sit well with me, but I knew if I didn't do as he said he'd most likely just drop me at home with instructions to stay put. Not wanting to sit home by myself, the best thing to do was to go along with Salinger's plan.

Feeling the need to do something with my time, I checked my emails while I waited for Salinger. There were several emails from online shopping outlets I frequented, as well as some e-cards from friends wishing me a merry Christmas. I scanned past an invitation to a New Year's Eve party as well as an online statement from the billing department at the hospital where I'd sent in a deposit for Catherine's birth. I was about to log off and check my Facebook page when a new email came through from Interested. He wanted to meet in a chat room so we could get to know each other, providing a link and asking me to join him there in two hours. I replied, saying I was anxious to get to know him as well. I logged off my email and was about to access Facebook when I saw Salinger leave the store.

"So?" I asked the minute he opened his door and slid into the driver's seat.

"The clerk said he didn't work that night, so he couldn't verify that Stella was in, but he confirmed she was a frequent customer."

"This store is pretty far from both her place of employment and her apartment. It seems there'd be more convenient stores from which to buy her alcohol."

"She may have been coming here for another reason," Salinger suggested. "Maybe a friend lives nearby."

"Maybe. Based on her log, she checked in at the truck stop out on the highway an hour before she stopped at the liquor store. Stella must have been at the truck stop for some reason, then stopped here on her way home."

"Sounds right."

"Does the store have a surveillance system?"

"It does, but the tapes are rewritten every third day, so the tape from the night Stella died is gone. The clerk gave me the phone number for the one who was working last Friday night. I'll see if he remembers seeing Stella. In the meantime, let's head over to the truck stop. Stella might have been there to buy gas, but if she went directly to the liquor store she must have gone into the restaurant. The truck stop and the liquor store are a five-minute drive apart; she had to have done something else in the hour between the check-ins."

"Maybe she met someone there," I suggested. "The bartender at Lucky's said Stella's phone dinged, she looked at it, and then left. We know she checked into Lucky's at six fifty-two. We don't know how long she stayed, but given her history of spending a lot of time there it seems reasonable she might have still been at Lucky's at around ten, when she received the message and left."

Salinger turned the key in the ignition and started the car. We didn't speak during the short drive, but when we arrived at the truck stop he once again instructed me to wait in the car. I wasn't thrilled to be left behind again but did as I was told.

I took out my phone and was about to check Facebook when I noticed someone walking out of the restaurant: a man who wore a blue uniform and looked like an employee. I watched as he smoked a cigarette and spoke on his phone. I was too far away to make out what he was saying, but he appeared to be having a casual conversation. I watched him toss his cigarette to the ground and stamp it out with his foot. Then he glanced at his watch and looked out at the highway. I had the sense he was about to head back inside when a dark sedan pulled into the lot and up to one of the gas pumps. The driver got out of his car and began to pump his gas. The man I'd been watching walked over to him and said a few words. The driver handed the guy what looked like a wad of money, and the restaurant employee pulled an envelope out of his pocket. He handed it to the driver, who glanced inside the envelope and nodded, and the man in the blue uniform walked away.

Chapter 8

"I'm almost positive I just saw a drug deal go down," I said to Salinger when he returned.

Salinger frowned. "A drug deal?"

"I saw a man in a blue uniform come out of the door to the restaurant and minimart," I began, and then explained everything I'd seen.

"I remember seeing the guy you're describing going in as I was coming out. Wait here. I'm going to see if I can track him down."

Great. It looked like I was back to waiting. I decided to call Jeremy to get an update on the reindeer situation. As of the end of the day yesterday there'd been just one reindeer left to find and return to the pen. I hoped he'd be able to manage that today; he was going out of town tomorrow and I wanted all the reindeer tucked back in before he left.

"Hey, Tiffany, it's Zoe," I said when she answered the phone at the Zoo.

"Zoe, how are you? How's the baby?"

"We're both fine. I'm looking for Jeremy. Is he around?"

"Yeah, hang on. I'll get him."

I listened to the carols that played while I was on hold. I couldn't believe it was only a few days until Christmas. Not only did I not feel ready, but somehow, I felt like the joy and fun of the season was slipping through my fingers. Hopefully, once Salinger and I solved this case and Zak got home the Christmassy feeling I'd enjoyed earlier in the month would return.

"Hey, Zoe; what's up?" Jeremy asked when he came on the line.

"I just wanted to see how we're doing with the last reindeer."

"I'm afraid Dasher is a tricky fellow. There've been a lot of sightings, but by the time we arrive at the location of the sighting the dude is gone. Based on the location of the sightings, it seemed he was on his way out of town, but then turned around and was heading back this way. Tank and Gunnar are on patrol and I'm hoping to return him to the pen by nightfall."

"Yeah, that would be ideal. Zak should be home sometime tomorrow and I'd like to have all the reindeer tucked back in before he gets here."

"We'll get him. I don't want you to worry about it at all. I know you've been helping Salinger, so just focus on the sleuthing and leave the reindeer roundup to me."

I wasn't sure I'd call doing what I'd been doing today sleuthing, but it beat the heck out of sitting home and *relaxing*, as everyone seemed to think I should be doing. As I've said on more than one occasion in recent days, sitting around and relaxing was for the birds.

"Okay, here's what I found out just now," Salinger said as he got back into the car. "The guy you saw works in the maintenance department at the truck stop. His name is David Gardner and he confirmed he knew Stella from when she stopped by for gas once a week, and they'd chat while she filled up her tank. I asked if she was in late last Friday and he said he worked the late shift but didn't remember seeing her."

"Why would Stella come all the way out here for gas when she lives and works in town, unless her real intention was to hook up with someone? Didn't her neighbor say she was seen heading out on a date with someone named David?"

"You're right, the neighbor did say that. Of course, David's a common name. I asked about the exchange you witnessed, and David said he'd picked up a video game for a friend and had arranged to get it to him and collect the money due him when he stopped for gas. There's no way to prove or disprove that, but I'm putting him on the suspect list."

"Okay. What now?"

"I'm going back to the office to make a few calls. I'll drop you back at home on the way."

"Oh, I almost forgot to tell you: I have a date to meet Interested in a chat room at four. Do you want me to handle it myself?"

"No. I'll come over to your place for the chat. I think we need to try to get him to commit to a meeting. When I'm face-to-face with him I can find out exactly how he's able to do what he's doing and whether he's a viable suspect in the murder investigation."

Ellie and Alex were in the kitchen making cookies when I got home. I poured myself a glass of milk, grabbed a couple of cookies, and sat down at the table. "How was shopping?" I asked.

"It was fun," Alex responded. "Eli loves all the bright lights and decorations. I love to see his eyes light up every time he spies something new."

"I talked to my mom this morning; she wants all of us to go into town together this evening to look at the windows and she's making a reservation for dinner. I was thinking around six. Do you think Levi and Scooter will be done by then?"

"The second shift is supposed to relieve Levi at five. I'll text him to let him know we're going out so he won't dawdle."

"Okay, great, I'll tell Mom we're on."

"It's too bad Zak isn't here," Alex commented. "He loves the windows."

"Yeah." I couldn't help but feel a little sad.

"Scooter will want to bring Tucker," Alex said. "In fact, he's planning to ask if he can spend the night. If you're okay with that you should include him as well."

"Yeah, I'm fine with it. I'll text him about what we're doing."

"Maybe you should take a nap in the meantime," Ellie suggested.

"I can't. I need to clean up and then I have a date in a Sexy Singles chat room at four."

Ellie gave me the oddest look, though she didn't respond. I was sure she was struggling for something to say.

"Salinger will be here at around three forty-five. He'll be coming along on the date."

"This has to do with the case you're working on?" Ellie said.

"Of course. Did you think I really had a date in a singles chat room?"

"Well, no, but…oh, never mind. If I see Salinger pull up I'll send him into the office."

I looked at Alex. "We might be able to use your help if you're game."

"Sure. Just let me know what you need me to do."

******

Salinger arrived at five minutes to four. I logged on to the computer, then followed the link Interested had provided to the chat room. Once there, I waited for him to make his appearance. At exactly four o'clock he logged on.

The conversation started off with him asking me about myself. I was careful to give answers that might persuade him to want to meet me while not giving away anything that might lead to my real identity. Alex had logged on to Zak's computer and was attempting to trace the location of the computer Interested was using.

"He's on a phone," Alex said after a few minutes, "registered to Roseanne Candlewood."

"Interested is female?" I asked.

"Not necessarily," Alex answered. "Sometimes cell phones on a family plan are all registered to the person who set it up. For example, if you traced my cell it would tell you it's registered to Zak

Zimmerman. Your phone would show the same thing, most likely."

"So maybe Interested is married to Roseanne Candlewood, who has the plan registered under her name," I said.

"Maybe," Alex replied. "Or maybe someone named Roseanne Candlewood really is interested in hooking up with Marilyn M."

"Either way, I just got Interested to agree to a meeting," Salinger said.

"Won't Interested know right away that something's off when you show up?" I asked.

"Yes, but I plan to identify Interested before he or she knows who I am or why I'm there."

How will I know who you are? Salinger typed.

I'll find you. I saw your photo on the dating website, so I know what you look like, Interested typed back.

"Uh-oh," I said aloud.

"I'll get one of the cops from Bryton Lake to show up at the meetup. There are a couple of women in that office who'll pass with a blond wig and a little makeup." Salinger closed the computer after confirming the time and place. "You go have fun with your family, and whatever you do, stay far, far away from Lucky's tonight."

"Is that where you're meeting?" I asked.

"It is, and I don't want to be worrying about you." Salinger looked at Alex. "Let everyone know Zoe isn't to leave the family group at any point during the evening. Maybe between all of you, you can manage to keep her out of my way."

"I'll make sure she stays with us," Alex answered.

Great. Now I was being babysat by my daughter.

******

"Oh, look at the ponies," my three-year-old sister Harper squealed.

"Those aren't ponies; they're reindeer like Zoe has at her house," my mom corrected her as we looked at the North Pole display in one of the windows.

It really was the perfect night. There were a few snow flurries in the air, which added to the holiday atmosphere, yet it wasn't windy, wet, or overly cold. The shops along Main Street were lit up with holiday lights, and each storefront had a special display. In the past the windows had been coordinated to tell a story, but this year the merchants association had decided to do away with the story and allow each shopkeeper to create their own display. The windows would be voted on during Hometown Christmas and the winning one would receive a trophy that could be displayed on their sales counter for the following year.

"Can we go ice skating?" Alex asked.

"I won't be able to go with you this year, but it's fine by me if you do," I answered.

"Me and Tucker want to go to the sledding hill," Scooter countered.

I glanced at Mom. "Actually, I was thinking of hot cocoa and vanilla ice cream," she answered my unspoken question.

"I'll take Alex ice skating," Ellie volunteered. "And Levi can take the boys sledding. If you'll take Eli to the ice cream shop with you, we can all meet back here in an hour or so."

"That sounds like a good plan," my mom said.

"I think I'm going to run down the street to the sporting goods store to look for some stocking stuffers for Zak," I commented as the group that included my mom, dad, sister, grandpa, Hazel, and Eli turned toward the ice cream shop.

Alex paused and looked at me with a worried expression on her face.

"Don't worry. I won't go anywhere near the bar. I promise. I just want to get a little last-minute shopping done."

"Pinky swear." Alex held up the little finger on her right hand.

"Pinky swear." I locked my pinky with hers.

"Okay. Be careful on the ice," Alex cautioned.

"I will. Have a good time. If I finish my errand in time I'll come over to watch you skate."

I felt bad that Alex felt she needed to worry about me. It was true I'd managed to get myself into some sticky predicaments in the past, but I had Catherine to worry about now, so I was determined to stick to my promise to be extra careful. As I walked down the street with my daughter doing a jig in my stomach, I let the festive atmosphere relax me. I couldn't help but smile as I paused to listen to a group of carolers dressed in Victorian costumes. I recognized several of them as being involved in Hometown Christmas from years past and realized they must be out doing a trial run.

"Zoe, is that you?"

I turned around and smiled at the woman who was hurrying down the sidewalk toward me. "Aspen," I greeted the kindergarten teacher and animal activist I hadn't seen for a couple of years. "How are you?"

"I'm good. I hadn't heard you were pregnant."

I placed my hand on my belly. "Aspen, meet Catherine."

"Your first?"

"Yes. She'll be our first biological child."

Aspen hugged me. "Congratulations. It looks like you're due soon."

"In a few weeks. So, how have you been?"

"I'm good. I moved away from Ashton Falls after the kitten incident, but I've decided to come back, so I'm here looking at rentals. I was originally going to head home tomorrow, but my friend's daughter is part of the parade tomorrow, so I'm staying an extra day. Is Zak here with you?"

"He's in Europe, but he'll be home tomorrow. I was just going to the sporting goods store. If you have time walk with me and we can catch up."

Aspen looked at her watch. "I'm supposed to meet my friend, but I have a few minutes."

I started walking and Aspen followed along.

"The town really went all-out with the decorations this year," Aspen commented.

"The events committee is hoping for an extra-good turnout for Hometown Christmas, so they asked the merchants to go all-out with the decorations and added a few things like the parade and reindeer exhibit."

"I was wondering what the pen in the park was for. You do know it's empty, right?"

I laughed. "I know. The reindeer are in a pen at my house until tomorrow. Once the reindeer are moved to the pen in the park there has to be twenty-four-hour security, so the committee decided to house them at a private residence until the event actually got started. Of course, in retrospect that may not have been the best choice; someone let them out of the pen, but Jeremy managed to round up all but one."

Aspen stopped walking. "I don't suppose you mean that one." She pointed to a reindeer standing next to the giant Christmas tree in the town square.

"Yes, I believe that's Dasher." Fortunately, although people were stopping to take photos of the animal, no one had approached him. "I need to call the Zoo. Hopefully, he won't take off before Jeremy gets here."

"I'll get him."

I watched as Aspen unwound a rope that was draped through green poles that were used to divide the sidewalk from the street. Once she had a length of it free, she slowly walked toward the animal, talking to it softly. I was sure the reindeer would take off as soon as he noticed Aspen approaching. I just hoped he wouldn't trample the people who'd gathered to watch in the process.

I held my breath as Aspen reached out a hand and petted the reindeer's face. She had the rope tied into a lasso, which she gently put over his head. Then she tied him to a nearby post and waved me over.

"Go ahead and call Jeremy. I think this guy is tired and ready to go home."

I called Jeremy and told him to bring the van, then turned to Aspen. "That was amazing. How did you do it?"

"I guess you could say I have a way with animals. This big guy could sense I meant him no harm. He was ready to go home, so he let me approach."

"Well, thank you. We've been trying to catch up with him all week."

Aspen shrugged. "No problem. I'll let my friend know I'm waiting with you for Jeremy to arrive."

"I appreciate that. If you ever need a job we could use someone like you at the Zoo."

"Actually, I will need a job once I've relocated."

"I'll text you my number. We can set up a time to talk after the first of the year."

"Thank you. I'd like that very much."

I was texting Aspen my number just as Jeremy pulled up with the van. She left to meet her friend as soon as Jeremy took over, but I stayed to make sure everything went off without a hitch.

"How did you manage to catch up with this wily creature?" Jeremy asked.

"I was talking to Aspen and we noticed him standing by the tree. Aspen grabbed a piece of the guard rope and walked right up to him. He just stood there while she slipped the rope over his neck and tied him to the post. It was amazing. I offered her a job. I probably should have discussed it with you first, but it was kind of a spur-of-the-moment thing."

"I think she'll fit right in and we will need the extra help. Tiffany wants to go to part time after she and Scott get married and I'm going to need to take some time off this summer when the new baby arrives."

"New baby?" I asked.

"I was supposed to wait to tell anyone until after the first of the year, but Jessica and I are expecting our first child together."

"Oh, wow. That's fantastic." I hugged Jeremy. "I'm sure Rosalie and Morgan will be thrilled to have a new baby in the house."

Rosalie was Jessica's daughter and Morgan was Jeremy's. With a third, shared child, they'd make the perfect blended family.

Jeremy got Dasher loaded up and I decided to head back to join the family. I didn't want them worrying about me if my errand was delayed. Alex and Ellie were still on the ice, but Levi and the boys must have finished sledding because they were having a snowball fight in a field nearby.

I felt a pain in my abdomen that took my breath away. I grabbed onto a tree and hung on until it passed. I'd had contractions off and on for the past week, but this one was a lot stronger and had lasted longer. Catherine must be as tired of waiting to be born as me.

Once the contraction passed I made my way over to a bench where I could watch Alex and Ellie gliding around the ice. I tried to maintain the holiday spirit I'd felt earlier in the evening, but sitting on the sidelines once again left me feeling angsty. I took out my phone to call Salinger to find out if he'd had his date with Interested and, if he had, whether he'd garnered any additional information that might solve Stella's murder.

Salinger answered after the first ring. "I was just about to call you."

"Do you have news?" I asked.

"In a way. It turns out Interested is a nineteen-year-old named Jared Candlewood. Roseanne is his mother and the phone he sent the email from is on her family plan, as Alex suggested."

I frowned. "Okay, so how did he get access to my email address through the dating site? I never agreed to a meet with anyone."

"Jared works for Data Tek Industries, a corporate computer system that includes the Sexy Singles dating site. He admitted he occasionally looked around while he was in the system doing updates and repairs. Marilyn isn't the first woman he's set up a date with using information he obtained illegally."

"The kid's nineteen. Do any of the women he approaches ever follow through with the date he sets up?"

"He said his success rate is about fifty percent. But that's not important. What is, is that Jared said he didn't send any emails to Stella, but he isn't the only technician working for Data Tek. He gave me the name and contact information for three other young men who would have had access to the computer system."

"Any of them have the initials DMG?"

"There's a Donald Goldberg. I'll start with him and then move on to the others if that doesn't yield me any results."

I gasped as another contraction gripped my stomach.

"Are you okay?" Salinger asked.

"Yeah, I'm fine. Catherine is just moving around a bit more than usual. It looks like my parents and the others are on their way here, so I should go. Call me tomorrow to let me know how your interviews turn out."

"I will, and you get some rest. The most important job you have now is taking care of your baby."

"I know and thanks."

I felt myself relax as the contraction eased. The doctor had said I'd have contractions leading up to the actual event and that as long as they were randomly spaced I shouldn't worry about them. Most of the ones I'd experienced had been minor in intensity, but the last couple had kicked it up a notch. Still, the contractions didn't seem to be coming on any sort of a regular time line, so I decided not to mention them to the others. The last thing I needed was a bunch of mother hens hovering over me.

Chapter 9

Friday, December 22

I woke the next morning to a text letting me know Zak was on his way home. He predicted he'd get into the airport at about the same time as Pi, so they'd ride up the mountain together. If all went as planned I should have my entire family home by six o'clock that evening. I couldn't help but smile at the thought of a good old-fashioned Christmas with everyone I loved. I'd hoped to have Stella's murder solved before now, but Salinger was correct when he said the most important thing was for me to provide a safe environment for my unborn child.

I pulled on a robe and slippers and went down the stairs. I could hear cartoons playing in the den, which probably meant Scooter and Tucker were up. When I entered the kitchen, which had been warmed by a cheery fire, I found Ellie feeding Eli while Alex frosted gingerbread men at the nearby counter.

"Something smells wonderful," I said as I made a cup of herbal tea.

"Gingerbread," Alex answered. "Ellie's donating them for the high school bake sale at Hometown Christmas. Are we going to the parade?"

"I planned on it. The parade is at five and Zak and Pi should be home at six, so I figured we'd go to the parade and then come home for dinner. If that's okay with everyone else, of course."

"Fine by me," Alex answered. "I miss Zak and I'm excited to see Pi." She looked at Ellie. "We should make a lasagna. Zak loves lasagna and we can make it ahead of time and then heat it up when we get home from the parade."

"That sounds like a wonderful idea," Ellie responded.

"Can I make you some breakfast?" Alex asked.

"I think I'm just going to have one of those cookies."

"Zak told me to make sure you eat healthy food, not just junk," Alex scolded.

"Fine." I sighed. "I'll have a couple of eggs, scrambled." At what point, I wondered, had Alex become the parent and I the child? "Is Levi at the tree lot?"

"Yeah, but he'll be getting off early because he's on the high school float," Ellie said. "He said he'd meet us at the parking area afterward. He also wanted me to let you know the Hometown Christmas crew will be by to pick up the reindeer at around noon. They have around-the-clock security scheduled until the event's over, and then they'll bring them back to you."

"I know Zak worked everything out before he left, so I'm sure it'll all be fine. I'm just glad we managed to get everyone back in the pen in time. It was touch-and-go for a while."

"Do you still think someone let them out intentionally?" Alex asked as she set a plate with scrambled eggs and whole-grain toast in front of me.

"I don't know. It seems likely the gate was left open intentionally, but I suppose it's possible I may not have latched it securely. I don't think we'll ever know for sure. As long as they're safe now, I guess it doesn't matter."

I tensed up as another contraction gripped my body.

"Are you okay?" Ellie asked.

"I'm fine. I'm just having a few random contractions. The doctor said they were to be expected during the last weeks."

"How often?" Ellie asked.

"Very random. I had several last night, but they were widely spaced and this was the first one I've had this morning. I'm totally fine. If they become more frequent I'll call the doctor. I promise."

"Okay. I had early labor beginning a couple of weeks before I gave birth as well, but it's better to be safe than sorry, so don't let it go too long if they begin to come in regular intervals."

"I won't." I pushed my empty plate aside. "I think I'll go up and get dressed. I want to call Salinger and I have a few more gifts to wrap this morning. Did Levi feed the reindeer?"

"He said everything was taken care of, so you don't need to do anything. He's even going to have

Jeremy come over to help with the transfer. All you need to do is relax and take it easy."

I wished everyone would stop telling me to relax and take it easy. I wasn't a take-it-easy sort of person. Sitting around waiting for Catherine to arrive was going to drive me crazy if I didn't keep busy.

After I showered and dressed I called Salinger. I was hoping he'd have a break in the case that would require my immediate attention.

"I was wondering when you'd call," Salinger greeted me.

"Alex made me eat a nutritious breakfast before I did anything else. Do you have news?"

"I do, but I'm afraid it isn't great news."

I sat down on the edge of the bed. "What do we know?"

"I managed to speak to Donald Goldberg. After a bit of persuasion he admitted to being DMG."

"So we found our guy."

"We found the guy who sent the emails. He came across Stella's account during a maintenance session. He was able to ascertain by the discussion in the chat rooms she frequented and the number and type of men she dated that she was in to some kinky stuff. Goldberg emailed her to try to get in on the action, but she shot him down. On several occasions he kept trying to persuade her, but she didn't budge. One of the guys she dated had mentioned in one of his online chat sessions that she was in to the dominatrix thing, so he decided to play the tough guy, changing his emails to reflect the new role to get her attention. She never agreed to a date and he never met her in person."

"He has to be lying."

"Maybe, but he has an alibi for the time of Stella's murder. Whatever the intention of his emails, he didn't kill her."

"So where does that leave us? You spoke to all seven men she dated as well as the person who was sending her threatening emails and we still have nothing."

"I'm beginning to think perhaps Stella's murder isn't related to the dating site at all. I think we should go back to looking at the events that occurred on the last day of her life. The texts she received, as well as the places we know she spent time."

I let out a long breath. "Okay. Where do we begin?"

"I think we need to go as far back in her day as we can to create a time map. I want to revisit her neighbors and the employees at the locations where she checked in. Stella was out and about on the night she died. Someone must have seen her. It's even possible someone we've already spoken to was lying."

"I want to help. Why don't you come over? That way if we need Alex to do the computer thing she'll be here to help."

"Okay. I'll be there in thirty minutes."

******

When Salinger showed up we went back through everything we had and tried to map her last day. Between the texts and emails she sent me, her own phone records, and the check-ins from her phone to her social media accounts, we had a good outline of where she'd been.

"Okay, here's what we have," I began. "Stella received an email from DMG at noon. She texted me at twelve-nineteen, asking me to call her. I was out shopping with Ellie, so I didn't notice the text or reply. At one o'clock on the dot she texted me again. This time she added that it was important I get back to her as soon as possible."

I paused and took a breath, desperately trying to squelch my feelings of guilt. After a few beats I continued. "At one-thirteen, Stella checked in from Rosie's. She must have gone over there right after texting me. At two-ten she left the first voice message on my phone, asking me if Zak could help her track the source of some emails she'd received. At that point I still hadn't seen my messages. Then, at four-forty, she received another email from DMG. At four fifty-seven she called me again, sounding much more desperate. I must have been on my way to the hospital by then. I didn't receive her messages until much later and even when I did, I didn't reply because I was in the hospital and had my own problems. Still, looking back, I really should have made the effort to call her. If I had she might still be alive."

"You don't know that," Salinger reminded me. "If the person who sent the emails didn't kill her, discovering his identity might not have made a bit of difference."

"Yeah, Zoe," Alex added. "It's not your fault."

I appreciated them trying to make me feel better, but somehow it wasn't working.

"So, what happened after she called you the second time?" Salinger asked.

"Stella checked in at Lucky's at six twenty-two. The next time we have any evidence of her movements is when she checked in at the truck stop at ten-fifteen."

"Wait," Alex said. "According to Stella's phone records, she had a text at nine fifty-eight."

"That must be the ding the bartender at Lucky's heard just before she left," I commented. "Do we know who the phone the text came from is registered to?"

"Hang on." Alex began typing. After a couple of minutes she said, "The phone is registered to David Gardner."

I glanced at Salinger, who was frowning. David Gardner was the man I'd seen making the exchange at the truck stop. "Say Gardner's a drug dealer, as I suspect. Could Stella have been at the bar waiting for the green light to meet up with him? Once she had her drugs she headed over to the liquor store, where she checked in at eleven twenty-two to pick up some booze to wash everything down."

"It does seem a likely scenario, but it still doesn't tell us who killed her," Salinger pointed out.

I sat back in my chair and considered the situation. "It seems like we need to speak to everyone with whom she came into contact on the last day of her life. We know she went to Rosie's. Maybe she met someone for lunch, and maybe that someone knows what Stella had on her mind. And then she went to Lucky's. I spoke to the bartender, but you might be able to get more out of him. And then we need to have another chat with David Gardner and the clerk at the liquor store."

"It sounds like a lot of running around," Salinger said.

"Then I guess we'd better get started." I looked at Alex. "I'll be home in time to go with everyone to the parade. Let Ellie know what I'm doing and make sure Scooter and Tucker are ready on time."

"Yeah, okay. But be careful."

I smiled at Alex. "Don't worry. Salinger won't let anything happen to me."

******

Salinger and I decided to start at Stella's apartment. He'd managed to interview most of her neighbors, but he'd never caught up with the man who lived in the first apartment at the top of the stairs. It seemed that out of all the residents he would have been in the best position to see everyone who lived on the second floor coming and going. This time he answered the door when Salinger knocked.

"Yeah?" he barked. He was unshaven and wearing nothing more than a bathrobe. It looked as if we'd woken him up.

"I'm Sheriff Salinger and this is Zoe. We're investigating the death of your neighbor, Stella Green, and would like to ask you a few questions."

"I don't know anything about her death. I worked the late shift that night. You can check with my employer."

I spoke up. "Living where you do, we hoped you might have seen people walking past your apartment. We're interested in people who might have visited Stella or been seen with her in the past few weeks of her life."

"Stella didn't have a lot of company. I guess there was a friend or two who would stop by, but I don't know their names."

"That's totally understandable." I smiled. "If it's all right I just want to show you a few photos and you can tell me if any of the men look familiar."

The man shrugged, so I pulled up the profiles of the seven men we knew Stella had dated on my phone. I showed her neighbor each photo individually and he didn't remember seeing any of them. It sort of made sense that if Stella was only looking for a one-night stand, she might have met the men wherever they were going rather than revealing where she lived.

"How about this one?" I showed him the photo of David Gardner.

"Yeah, I've seen him a time or two. I think he and Stella are friends."

"And how about him?" I pulled up a photo I'd got off the internet of Donald Goldberg, the man who'd sent the emails.

"Nope, he doesn't look familiar."

"And him?" I showed him a photo of Docker.

"Yeah. He's been here. Last time I saw him he was with his friend. Can't say I remember either man's name."

"Did any of the other people in the building have a problem with Ms. Green?" Salinger asked.

"Not that I know of. She liked to keep to herself and usually didn't make a lot of noise."

"If you think of anything else call me." Salinger handed him a card.

I turned to Salinger when we returned to the car and he was inserting the key in the ignition. "What do you think?"

"Seems he wants to be left alone and out of things, but I didn't get the feeling he was holding anything back. We know the neighbor beneath Stella heard her arguing with someone on the night she died, but even she said it was unusual for Stella to have guests, that Stella went out a lot but rarely had people in. The only person I know of who visited her in the two weeks before her death was someone named David, who could have been her dealer, and a tall man with dark hair, both seen by the man we just spoke to and the neighbor at the other end of the walkway."

"So, on to Rosie's?" I asked.

"Seems like our best bet."

By the time Salinger and I arrived there the first lunch guests had begun to arrive. We sat down in a booth in the back and asked to speak to the waitress who'd served Stella the previous Friday. The hostess wasn't sure who that was off hand, but she promised to ask around and get back to us. We both asked for glasses of water while we waited.

"I guess our timing wasn't the best," I said as the tables filled up. Not only was it lunchtime but it was a Friday, which was normally a busier day, and the last Friday before the Christmas weekend. Based on the fact that a lot of patrons held brightly wrapped packages, there were going to be a lot of office get-togethers going on that afternoon.

After about five minutes a waitress named Roni Westbrook approached our table. I knew her fairly well because she'd worked at Rosie's back when it had been owned by Ellie's mom and she'd worked there too.

"I hear you want to ask some questions about Stella Green," Roni said.

"She checked in from here last Friday and we're trying to retrace her steps for the day," I explained.

"Do you remember seeing her?" Salinger asked the more direct question.

"She was here," Roni said. "It was a busy day, so I can't tell you the exact time, but I remember her being here with a friend."

"Do you know the friend?" Salinger asked.

"Some guy named David. I don't know him, though he looked sort of familiar. I think he might live in town, but he isn't a regular at Rosie's."

"Did it seem like they were pals or was it more of a business lunch?" I asked.

"Strictly personal. If you ask me, from the hand-holding and intimate looks, they were sleeping together. Although, now that I think about it, there seemed to be something else going on. At least at first."

"Can you elaborate?" Salinger asked.

"Stella got here first. She sat down at a table and ordered coffee. She seemed withdrawn and looked sort of," Veronica paused, as if searching for the right word, "haunted. She had dark circles under her eyes and it looked like she'd lost a lot of weight since I'd seen her only a couple of weeks earlier. I even worried she might be sick, but then I realized she was probably just using again."

"Using?" Salinger asked.

"Normally I wouldn't rat out a friend, but because she's dead and all I don't suppose it could hurt. Stella has had an on-again, off-again love affair with amphetamines for years now. It seemed like she was doing better and had gotten her life together, but from the way she looked last Friday I'm not so sure that was true at all."

"Did you speak with her when she was here?" I asked.

"No. Like I said, it was busy. She told me that her friend David was meeting her and to show him to the table when he arrived. When I checked back on her a little while later he was sitting with her and they were whispering. She had a serious look on her face and looked upset, but then he whispered something in her ear and she smiled. After that they were all lovey-dovey. Other than to take their order and bring them the check, I didn't speak to them at all."

"Did Ms. Green come in often?" Salinger asked.

Roni shrugged. "I guess it depends on how you define often; she usually came in once a week or so." Veronica looked over her shoulder. "Listen, I need to get back to my tables. I wish I had more to offer. Suzie Quinn is off today, but she worked last Friday and I saw her stop by the table and chat with Stella and David for a few minutes. You can call her to see if she has anything to add."

"I'll need the phone number," Salinger said.

"Sure, no problem. I'll get it."

Roni came back with the phone number and we went out to Salinger's car. He called Suzie and learned David was not only a friend of Stella's but her dealer. She confirmed David worked at the truck stop and, based on the description provided, the maintenance worker I'd seen outside.

"Back to the truck stop?" I asked.

"Yeah, although we don't have any proof David sold drugs to Stella or anyone else. My gut says he isn't going to talk unless we have a way to persuade him to do so."

"Then what do we do?"

"I'm thinking we need to set up a buy. David seemed like a low-level player. My impression is, he does a few deals here and there to make some extra spending money. If we can catch him in the act I think he'll be easily persuaded to tell us what we need to know about Stella's movements and his involvement in them on the night she died."

"What if he killed her?" I asked.

"Why would he? As far as I can tell, he didn't have a motive. He seems to have drugs to sell and Stella seemed to want to buy them. That's a pretty symbiotic relationship to me."

"You said earlier in the week that one of Stella's neighbor's saw her going on a date with someone named David. David also had lunch with her. I don't know much at all about drug deals, but I don't think dealers usually have lunch with their clients. And Roni did say it appeared they were sleeping together. Maybe David wasn't just a dealer. Maybe he was a boyfriend and there was jealousy involved in whatever went down that night."

Salinger slid his key in the ignition. "I guess you have a point. Let's head out to the truck stop. If we're lucky a good bluff might persuade David to tell us what he knows and we won't need to get the county drug unit involved."

Once again, Salinger instructed me to stay in the car when we arrived. Color me bored, although sitting on the sidelines of Salinger's investigation was better than sitting at home doing nothing. Though I supposed if I'd chosen to stay home today rather than go sleuthing with Salinger, Ellie and Alex would have done something creative to keep me occupied. I hated being a burden on those I loved, but it seemed that was what I'd been lately. Or maybe I just had a case of the baby bump blues, which, as I'd found out over the past eight months, had a way of making everything seem worse than it really was.

I checked my emails and phone messages while I waited. Other than a text from my mom, confirming our plans for the Christmas parade, there wasn't a lot going on in the phone and text department. Jeremy had left for his trip to visit Jessica's family, but before doing so he'd sent me a long email explaining what was going on in the Zoo and elsewhere. He'd helped move the reindeer to the new location before he left and assured me the town had a good plan to monitor and care for the large animals. He updated me on both the domestic and wild residents at the Zoo, and assured me that he had the staffing worked out for the duration of his absence. He wished me happy holidays and cautioned me to slow down and enjoy it. I sent a return email thanking him and wishing him happy holidays as well. I was about to look for some music to listen to when I felt another sharp pain in my abdomen. I felt my breath stall and my muscles tighten as the pain increased. After a minute or so it dissipated. I was about to return to my quest for the perfect playlist for a murder investigation when I saw Salinger walking toward me.

"That was fast," I said as he slipped into the car.

"That's because I was able to convince David it was in his best interest to cooperate. After a bit of persuasion he admitted Stella had been using amphetamines again and she'd picked up some drugs on Friday night."

"So, do we assume Stella came to the truck stop on the night she died to pick up the drugs she most likely requested while having lunch with David?"

"That matches what he said. Stella contacted her 'dealer' to put in an order earlier in the day. She received a text to meet him at the truck stop, where the exchange was to take place. Drugs in hand, she headed to the liquor store. David never admitted to being the dealer she hooked up with, but it seems obvious he was. He said he never saw her again after she left with the drugs that night."

"Do you believe him?"

Salinger shrugged. "I don't know. David's statement was vague by design, but it seems to me if he killed her he wouldn't have said anything at all. He admitted they went out sometimes and considered her to be a friend. Somehow, the way he said it rang true."

I sat back in the seat and let out a long sigh. "What now?"

"I'm not sure. I feel like we have a good idea of what Stella did on the last day of her life, but we haven't been able to place her with anyone at the very end of it. I think I'm going to go back to the office, look over my notes, and maybe make some calls. I have a feeling there's something I'm missing. I'll drop you back at home."

I was about to argue about the going-home part when another contraction grabbed me.

"You okay?" Salinger asked.

"Fine. Just tired, I guess. I think I'll take a nap before the parade."

Chapter 10

Zak called to let me know his plane had landed on time and he was going to meet Pi, whose plane was due to touch down within the next thirty minutes; then both of them would drive home. I told him that we were going to the parade but planned to have dinner at home. If he got into town early enough he said he'd meet me in town; if not he'd see us when we got home. Having Zak home was doing a lot to improve my mood, which even I had to admit had been on the grumpy side lately.

The first thing our little group did upon arriving in town was to check out the reindeer display to make sure they were tucked in nice and comfy. There was already a large crowd gathered around the reindeer, who'd become the stars of Hometown Christmas, but they looked both comfortable and secure, so I set worry aside and focused on watching the parade with my family.

The town had done a good job recruiting residents to participate despite the flurries in the air. Everyone was wrapped up in heavy winter wear, but the combination of festive floats, colorful decorations, sleigh rides, and curbside vendors selling hot cocoa and sweet snacks gave the town the feel of a real Christmas village.

"Doggies," Harper said when the Zoe's Zoo float, which Tiffany and Jeremy had built and Tank and Gunnar were driving, slowly made its way along the parade route.

"You did such a great job," Mom said as Dad picked Harper up to prevent her from running into the street to get a closer look at the animals on our float.

"I wish I could take credit, but it was the staff who handled it from planning to execution. It's pretty awesome, though."

The front of the float looked like a park and featured stuffed dogs playing on the lawn and stuffed cats sitting on the benches, while the back was meant to look like a forest filled with creatures from bears to squirrels. Jeremy had done a great job designing something that truly exemplified Zoe's Zoo.

The next float had been built by the staff at Bears and Beavers, a touristy type shop selling everything you could imagine that featured those animals. It replicated a small lake with a beaver dam with a single black bear drinking from the water.

"Here comes the high school group." Ellie pointed down the street. Eli screamed with delight when the band marched by, followed by the float, which featured elves in Santa's workshop. Levi, dressed as Santa, was sitting on a throne watching over his elves, all hard at work.

I felt another twinge in my abdomen as the float from Outback Hunting and Fishing approached. Feeling slightly dizzy, I decided I needed to sit down.

"I need to run to the bathroom," I said to Ellie. "It looks like the parade is winding down. I'll just meet you at the car."

Ellie gave me an odd look. "Are you okay?"

"I'm fine. Catherine's just kicking me in an uncomfortable spot."

Ellie smiled. "I remember those days." She handed me the keys to her car. "If you get there first go ahead and get in. Levi has another set if we get there first."

I took the keys. "Okay, thanks."

The town had set out several porta-potties for the event that I had absolutely zero intention of using. A lot of the stores were closed during the parade, but most would reopen afterward. I figured Mulligan's Bar and Grill would have stayed open throughout, so I headed in that direction. Not only would they have a clean bathroom but there'd most likely be somewhere to sit for a minute.

Fortunately, everyone was at the parade, so the place was empty. Even the bartender was nowhere to be found. I used the ladies' room and was walking back to the door when another contraction gripped my body. There was a booth nearby, so I decided to sit down for a minute to wait it out. The pain was just beginning to dissipate when Cory Wood came in from the back room. I was about to say hi when I had the oddest feeling. Normally, I'd attribute it to Zodar, but I wasn't entirely sure it wasn't just labor pains.

"Hi, Cory," I said as he stopped a few feet from where I was sitting.

He turned in my direction, appearing surprised to see me sitting there. "Zoe. Why are you in here all by yourself?"

"Just resting."

"I hear yah, man. It's crazy out there."

"Are you working at the bar?" I asked.

"Just for a couple of hours. The regular bartender is a friend of mine, and he wanted to take his kid to the parade, so I offered to cover. Easy way to make a buck. You're the first person to come in since the parade began. Do you want a drink?"

"No, I'm fine. I just needed a place to sit for a minute."

Cory pulled a packet of candy out of his pocket. "Skittles?"

"It seems you have quite the sweet tooth. Weren't you eating M&M pancakes when Jeremy and I stopped by to speak to you?"

Cory shrugged. "What can I say? I have a fondness for small, colorful bursts of flavor. You ever find out what happened to Stella?"

I pursed my lips. "No. Not yet. But Sheriff Salinger has some leads."

"Well, I hope you find the guy." He started to walk away.

"Wait," I said as an idea I hated to even explore popped into my mind. "Before you go, I do have one question for you."

Cory slid into the booth across from me. "Okay, shoot. I think I already told you everything I know, but if I can help…"

"One of Stella's neighbors said she saw you in the building late the night she died. After midnight," I bluffed. "I didn't remember whether you mentioned that when we spoke before."

"What neighbor?" Cory asked, a tone of suspicion in his voice.

I paused. I didn't know the name of any of the neighbors except Christopher, but it seemed risky to do any name-dropping.

"Who said they saw me at Stella's?" Cory asked again.

I decided to stick with a vague reply. "I'm not sure. Salinger told me that one of the neighbors told him that they saw you at Stella's on the night she died."

"It's seems odd you didn't mention that before."

"I didn't find out about it until after we spoke. Is there a problem?"

Cory popped a handful of Skittles into his mouth. "No problem. If you must know, I went over there to apologize for the fight we'd had the night before. Like I said, we'd been friends for a lot of years. I didn't want to leave it that way. We had a nice talk and mended fences and then I left."

"I guess that explains it." I started to get up. "I should get back to my friends. Have a nice night."

I left the bar and headed toward the car. The Skittle I'd found under the chair and the freshly vacuumed floor suggested Cory had been at Stella's on the night she died, that he'd spilled his candies and then someone had vacuumed them up. It could have gone down as Cory said—he'd shown up, spoken to her, and then left—but my Zodar was tingling. I felt sure now that Cory had been the one who'd killed Stella. But why? He'd said he'd been a friend of her brother and had known Stella for a long time. I knew he'd helped get her the job at the holiday store and he'd admitted to scooping Stella up and taking her home when he'd found her wasted at Lucky's. On the surface, it seemed he really cared for her, so why was my gut telling me that he was the killer we were looking for?

I reached Ellie's van, opened the passenger door, and slipped inside, then pulled out my phone to call Salinger. He didn't answer, so I decided to leave a message. "Hey, Salinger, it's Zoe. I think I know who killed Stella. I haven't worked out the why yet, but my gut…"

I paused as the driver's side door opened. My smile faded when I realized it was Cory and not Ellie who'd entered the vehicle.

"What are you doing here?" I asked.

"Something about our conversation struck me as strange. I realized it might behoove me to follow up."

"Strange how?"

"It was just a vibe. When I saw you were heading to the parking area and not back to your friends as you said in the bar, I thought I should follow to see what you were up to."

I felt my heart begin to pound. "I was tired and needed to rest. There's nothing strange going on."

Cory reached over and took the phone from my hand. He clicked it off, then tossed it out the window. "I heard you on the phone with the sheriff. I'm afraid it wouldn't be in my best interest to let you finish that call."

Cory grabbed the keys, which I'd left on the center console. He slid them into the ignition and started the van.

"What are you doing?" I screeched as he pulled out of the parking lot and on to the highway. A contraction gripped me and I gasped as the pain seared through my body. Cory stared intently at the road, not seeming to notice. "Where are you going?" I asked when Cory didn't answer.

"I don't know. Stop talking. I need to think."

"I don't know what you're thinking, but I don't know anything. Please stop the car. I think I'm in labor. I should get to the hospital."

Cory remained silent as he kept his eyes on the road ahead of us. I didn't know where he was driving, but I had a bad feeling about it. Another contraction gripped me as he maneuvered around a tight curve that caused me to slam into the door on my right side.

"I didn't kill her. At least not on purpose," Cory eventually said in a voice so soft I could barely make out his words. "Stella wasn't an easy person to love," he continued when I didn't reply. "She had such a beautiful spirit, but she seemed to forever be heading for the ultimate high or the deepest low. She never could find and maintain any sort of balance in her life." I saw a tear slide down his cheek. "I tried to help her. I really did. When she lost her job I helped her find a new one, and when she was passed out in her own vomit I cleaned her up. She said she wanted to change and I thought we might have a future together, but it was just an illusion. All those nights when I thought she was at Narcotics Anonymous meetings she was out prostituting herself with men she met online."

"I guess that must have made you angry," I said after a moment.

"It did. But I still loved her."

Cory had slowed the van as he'd begun to express his feelings. It might be a good idea to keep him talking. "So what happened?"

Cory frowned but didn't answer.

"I can tell you really cared about Stella. Maybe I can help."

"How can you help?" Cory demanded.

"I'm not sure, but Sheriff Salinger and I are friends. He'll listen to me, but first you need to tell me what happened."

I didn't think he was going to tell me the rest, but after a moment he began to speak again. "As you already know, Stella and I argued on Thursday night. I was usually able to maintain my calm when dealing with her because she was a fragile little thing, but that night I lost it. I never touched her except to force her into the car, but I said some mean things. I knew I'd hurt her and wanted to apologize, so I went over to her place the next night. She was totally wasted. Pills, booze, the whole nine yards. It suddenly hit me that she was never going to change. She was never going to be the woman I needed her to be. I started yelling and she started crying. She slapped me and I shoved her. She fell and hit her head. I was going to call 911, but when I realized she was dead I panicked and ran."

He pulled up in front of a cabin that had been built on a large lot just outside of town. "Where are we?" I asked.

"My place."

Cory got out of the van and walked around to the passenger side door. "Get out," he said.

"Why? What are you going to do with me?"

"I don't know; just get out."

I wanted to resist, but I was in no shape to engage in a physical altercation, so I did as he said. Cory told me to sit in a chair near the door, then used the cord from the miniblinds to bind my hands to it. Another contraction, the strongest so far, gripped me as he headed down the hallway. It seemed to me he'd gone into what must be his bedroom.

"Not now, baby," I whispered to Catherine. There was no way I wanted to give birth while tied to a chair in a filthy cabin with a man who very well might be planning to kill me.

A few minutes later, he came out carrying an overnight bag.

"Are you going somewhere?" I asked as another contraction caused my entire body to stiffen.

"I need to get out of town while I still can. Don't worry; my roommate will be home in about four hours. He'll set you free. Just relax in the meantime."

"I think I might be in labor. I don't know if I have four hours. Please, you have to let me go now. I won't tell anyone what happened with Stella."

"Good try, but you already told me you aren't due for a few weeks. Four hours will fly by if you just relax and stop fighting the ropes."

"But…" I said as the door slammed behind him. I heard the engine of the van come to life as he sped away.

I took several deep breaths, trying to steady the panic that was building inside. I'd been in sticky situations in the past and this was a mild predicament compared to some of them. Four hours wasn't all that long to wait. I was fairly comfortable and just needed to relax.

And then another contraction tore through my body. I panted through it and then looked at my watch. I'd been having contractions for a while now and they seemed to be getting both harder and closer together. When the next one gripped me, I realized they were now only three minutes apart.

"Please, Catherine. You need to wait, baby. I don't see how you can come into the world while I'm tied to a chair. Please, please, wait a while longer."

Tears streamed down my face as another contraction grasped me. I was never going to make it. The contractions were coming closer together. I had to find a way to get out of this chair. I pulled at the ropes, but Cory had tied them securely. I felt as if my body was being ripped apart as another contraction took hold. I screamed, although I knew there was no one to hear. I was sure I'd pass out from the pain when the front door flew open.

"Catherine's coming," I shouted to Salinger, who was untying the ropes around my hands.

"Don't worry. We'll get you to the hospital."

Salinger picked me up and carried me to his squad car. He placed me gently on the backseat, then turned on the lights and sirens and sped toward the hospital. He must have called ahead because there was a nurse with a wheelchair waiting when we arrived. Once I was settled into it, Salinger grabbed my hand. "You're in good hands now."

"Cory Wood killed Stella. He's in Ellie's van."

"I figured that much out. Zak, Ellie, and your mom are on the way. I'm going after Cory."

Salinger leaned forward and hugged me. Okay, that was a first, but I hugged him back before he jogged back to his squad car and drove away.

"Let's get you inside," the nurse said. "It looks like your baby is determined to be here for Christmas."

After a quick exam in the emergency room they took me directly to delivery.

"Zak. My husband. He was on his way. He should be here. I need him to be here."

The doctor looked at one of the nurses. "See if you can track down Mr. Zimmerman. And hurry. This baby is ready to be born."

The nurse left to find Zak and the doctor began to explain everything that was going to happen and what he needed me to do. "You're going to begin to have the urge to push, but don't do it. Not yet. I just want you to pant and try to relax through the contraction."

Relax? Was this guy kidding me?

"Okay, here comes a big one," the doctor said. "Pant and relax."

The panting was doable, the relaxing not so much, but I tried. The doctor was doing something down there, but I couldn't see his hands, so I wasn't sure what was going on.

"You can push with the next contraction," the doctor said.

"Zak. He should be here."

"On his way," one of the nurses said.

"Okay, now," the doctor said. "Push through the entire contraction."

I tried to do as the doctor said, but midway through, the push turned into a scream. I felt someone grab my hand and squeeze it tight. The pain was overwhelming, and I found my energy waning, but I could hear Zak's voice in my ear, encouraging me to hang in there just a little longer. I took a deep breath and pushed again.

"I have her now; pant," the doctor said as I felt Catherine slide from my body.

"Is she okay?" I asked as I tried to both relax and pant.

"She's perfect," Zak said in my ear.

I felt a drop of moisture on my shoulder. I glanced behind me to find tears streaming down my big, strong husband's face. I wanted to say something, but I was too exhausted to form words, so I just smiled. Zak smiled back and then he leaned over and kissed me gently on the forehead.

"Would you like to hold your daughter?" the nurse asked a few minutes later.

"Yes."

The back of the bed was raised, and the nurse handed me a still-wet baby wrapped in a white sheet. I cradled her in my arms as tears began to stream down my own face.

"She looks just like I imagined she would," I whispered as Zak shifted slightly so he was sitting by my side instead of at my head.

Zak wrapped his arms around both of us, and together we sobbed in happiness and relief.

Chapter 11

Sunday, December 24

I woke to the feeling of someone licking my face. I slowly opened my eyes to find Charlie next to me. It was still dark, so I knew it must be early, but Zak's side of the bed was empty. I glanced at the bassinette to find it empty as well.

"Zak?" I called softly so as not to wake the rest of the family.

"I'm here on the sofa."

I climbed out of bed and slipped on my robe. I crossed the room to find Zak sitting on the sofa of our seating area with Catherine sleeping peacefully in his arms.

"She was a little fussy and I didn't want to wake you."

I sat down next to Zak and laid my head on his shoulder. The room was lit by only the flames from the fireplace and the lights from the tree Zak had placed in the corner. Charlie jumped up onto the sofa next to me and laid his head in my lap. We'd decided to let Charlie get used to Catherine before we introduced her to the other resident animals, so Marlow and Spade were sleeping with Alex and Bella was sleeping with Scooter and Digger.

"Do you think she's hungry?" I asked as I marveled at the perfection that was our daughter.

"No. She needed to be changed and then she went right back to sleep. Based on the schedule the doctor gave us, she isn't due for a feeding for another hour. You should try to get some sleep. We have a busy day ahead of us."

I pulled a blanket over me and snuggle up closer to Zak. Charlie shifted as well, so I was surrounded by the comfort of those who loved me the most. "I love this. Sitting here with you and Catherine and Charlie in a dark house on Christmas Eve. It feels absolutely perfect."

Zak turned and gently kissed my lips. "It is pretty perfect, isn't it?"

I fixed my gaze on Catherine, with her thick head of dark hair and deep blue eyes. If the painting I had seen was accurate, the ancestor Catherine was named for had been a beautiful woman. Tall and regal with dark hair, blue eyes, clear pale skin, and a smile that seemed to light up a room.

"I'm sorry I worried you," I said after a while. "I really did try to stay out of trouble, but trouble seems to find me no matter what."

"I'll admit the hour between when Salinger called me to let me know he'd received a call from you that had been cut off and the time I finally laid eyes on you in the hospital was one of the worst of my life."

I closed my eyes and cringed. "I know. I'm sorry again. I don't want to worry you. I'm really going to try to change."

Zak shifted Catherine to his other arm and placed the arm closest to me around my shoulders. "As much as I don't want you to be in danger ever again, I don't want you to change. I love you just the way you are. I may have to hire a bodyguard to accompany you every time you leave the house for my own piece of mind, but I don't want you to try to become anyone other than who you are."

I hoped Zak was kidding about the bodyguard, but the rest of what he'd said warmed my heart.

I hadn't spoken to Salinger since he'd dropped me at the hospital. "Do you know if Salinger caught up with Cory?" I asked.

"He did. It might not have felt like one, but it was a stroke of luck that Cory took Ellie's van. It's equipped with an emergency locator. Salinger was able to check the system and not only see where Cory was but where he'd been. That's how he found you at Cory's house and how he eventually caught up with him when he tried to leave the state."

"Wow, way to go, modern technology."

"I'm very grateful Levi got the full upgrade package when he bought Ellie's van."

"Yeah, me too. It was pretty dicey there for a while. I was so worried Catherine would come before anyone found me."

Zak squeezed my shoulder with his free hand. I know he'd been as scared as I was and I felt bad for putting him through that.

"It looks like Catherine's waking up," Zak said after a moment. "I don't suppose it will hurt to feed her a little early, then maybe we can all get some sleep before your parents show up for breakfast."

Zak settled me into a chair with a pillow to support my arm. He carefully handed me Catherine as I helped her to settle on to my breast.

"I wasn't sure if we should continue with our Christmas Eve and Christmas Day plans, but Ellie and Levi agreed to stay here at the house through Christmas, and I know my parents are superexcited to spend time with Catherine."

"It'll be fine," Zak said. "Ellie is taking care of all the cooking and all three kids have volunteered to pitch in as well. You just need to promise me to take a nap if you start to feel tired. I don't want you overdoing it."

"I'll take it easy." I glanced down at Catherine, who seemed to be alternating between eating and sleeping. I caressed her cheek with my finger. "I'm excited for Christmas, but I think this will be the moment I look back on for years to come."

"It is pretty wonderful," Zak agreed.

"I guess it's a good thing my mom went ahead and bought Catherine the newborn-size First Christmas onesies."

"I'll dress her in one after I change her in the morning," Zak offered. "Do you want the red one with the white reindeer or the white one with the candy canes?"

"Either is fine. She can wear one today and one tomorrow." I smiled at my daughter. "It looks like she's gone back to sleep."

"I'll take her," Zak said as he got up and lifted her into his big, strong arms. She was so tiny and he was so big. I knew he would move heaven and earth if he had to, to keep her safe and happy.

After he changed her once again and settled her into the bassinette, he carried me to bed and lay down next to me. I listened to his heartbeat as he gathered me into his arms and we drifted off to sleep. I knew Zak and I would share many amazing Christmas Eves with each other and our family as it grew, but I also knew I would always remember the perfection of this magical night as Zak, Catherine, Charlie, and I welcomed the magic of our first Christmas as a family in a dark room lit only by the fire and the tree.

Recipes

Candied Cherry Slices—submitted by Vivian Shane
Cherry Coffee Cake—submitted by Darla Taylor
Marie's Minty Chocolate Chip Cookies—submitted by Marie Rice
Magic Cookie Bars—submitted by Pam Curran

Candied Cherry Slices

Submitted by Vivian Shane

An old recipe passed down from my grandmother.
Always a tradition for me to make at Christmas.

1 cup butter
1 cup sifted powdered sugar
1 egg
1 tsp. vanilla
2¼ cups sifted flour
1 cup pecans
2 cups candied cherries (cut in quarters)

Cream butter and powdered sugar. Blend in egg and
vanilla. Add flour and mix well. Stir in pecans and
cherries. Chill one hour. Divide into thirds and shape
into rolls. Wrap in wax paper and chill 3 hours. Cut
into 1/8″ slices. Bake on ungreased cookie sheets at
325 degrees for 12–15 minutes or until delicately
browned on edges.

Cherry Coffee Cake

Submitted by Darla Taylor

½ cup butter (1 stick), softened
2 cups sugar
4 eggs
2 cups flour
2 tsp. baking powder
½ tsp. salt
1 21-oz. can Lucky Leaf Cherry or Sweet Dark
Cherry Fruit Filling
1 cup confectioners' sugar
4 tsp. water
2 tsp. vanilla

Preheat oven to 350 degrees.

Cream butter and sugar; beat in eggs, one at a time.

Stir in flour, baking powder, and salt.

Pour into greased 9 x 13-inch pan.

Spoon fruit filling over top, swirl.

Bake 40 minutes until golden.

Cool. Blend confectioners' sugar with water and
vanilla, then drizzle over cake.

Marie's Minty Chocolate Chip Cookies

Submitted by Marie Rice

Back before there was such a thing as mint chocolate chips (gasp!), I came up with this idea in high school. I wanted to add a peppermint taste to my chocolate chip cookies, specifically for making Christmas cookies.

2¼ cups all-purpose flour
1 tsp. baking soda
2 sticks (1 cup) butter, softened
¾ cup sugar
¾ cup brown sugar
1 tbs. cinnamon
½ tsp. vanilla extract
½ tsp. peppermint extract
2 eggs
12-oz. pkg. semisweet chocolate chips

Preheat oven to 350 degrees.

In a small bowl, mix together flour and baking soda; set aside. In a large bowl, cream together butter, sugars, cinnamon, and extracts until smooth. Add eggs one at a time, beating well after each. Gradually beat in flour mixture. Stir in the chocolate chips.

Lightly spray baking sheets. Drop rounded teaspoonfuls onto the sheets. Bake on middle or upper rack for approximately 10 minutes or until golden brown and no longer wet. (This will vary from oven to oven. Each oven I've used has needed a slightly different amount of time to cook thoroughly without burning the bottoms.)

Cool for a couple of minutes on baking sheet and then move cookies to cooling rack to finish cooling (if they last that long!). If reusing the baking sheet for another batch, use spatula to scrap the sheet and then respray before placing more cookie dough on the sheet.

Notes:

* For a stronger mint taste, replace the vanilla extract with more peppermint extract.
* Mint chocolate chips can also replace the semisweet chocolate chips.

Magic Cookie Bars

Submitted by Pam Curran

These are yummy and rich.

½ cup margarine or butter
1½ cups graham cracker crumbs
1 14-z. Eagle Brand Sweetened Condensed Milk (not evaporated milk)
1 6-oz. pkg. semisweet chocolate morsels
1⅓ cups coconut
1 cup chopped nuts

Preheat oven to 350 degrees. In a 9 x 13-inch baking pan, melt margarine in oven. Sprinkle crumbs over margarine; mix together and press into pan. Pour sweetened condensed milk evenly over crumbs. Top evenly with remaining ingredients; press down firmly. Bake 25–30 minutes or until lightly browned. Cool thoroughly before cutting. Store loosely covered at room temperature.

Books by Kathi Daley

Come for the murder, stay for the romance.

Zoe Donovan Cozy Mystery:
Halloween Hijinks
The Trouble With Turkeys
Christmas Crazy
Cupid's Curse
Big Bunny Bump-off
Beach Blanket Barbie
Maui Madness
Derby Divas
Haunted Hamlet
Turkeys, Tuxes, and Tabbies
Christmas Cozy
Alaskan Alliance
Matrimony Meltdown
Soul Surrender
Heavenly Honeymoon
Hopscotch Homicide
Ghostly Graveyard
Santa Sleuth
Shamrock Shenanigans
Kitten Kaboodle
Costume Catastrophe
Candy Cane Caper
Holiday Hangover
Easter Escapade
Camp Carter
Trick or Treason
Reindeer Roundup

Zimmerman Academy The New Normal
Ashton Falls Cozy Cookbook

Tj Jensen Paradise Lake Mysteries by Henery Press:

Pumpkins in Paradise
Snowmen in Paradise
Bikinis in Paradise
Christmas in Paradise
Puppies in Paradise
Halloween in Paradise
Treasure in Paradise
Fireworks in Paradise
Beaches in Paradise – *June 2018*

Whales and Tails Cozy Mystery:

Romeow and Juliet
The Mad Catter
Grimm's Furry Tail
Much Ado About Felines
Legend of Tabby Hollow
Cat of Christmas Past
A Tale of Two Tabbies
The Great Catsby
Count Catula
The Cat of Christmas Present
A Winter's Tail
The Taming of the Tabby
Frankencat
The Cat of Christmas Future
The Cat of New Orleans – *February 2018*

Seacliff High Mystery:

The Secret
The Curse
The Relic
The Conspiracy
The Grudge
The Shadow
The Haunting

Sand and Sea Hawaiian Mystery:

Murder at Dolphin Bay
Murder at Sunrise Beach
Murder at the Witching Hour
Murder at Christmas
Murder at Turtle Cove
Murder at Water's Edge
Murder at Midnight

Writers' Retreat Southern Mystery:

First Case
Second Look
Third Strike
Fourth Victim
Fifth Night – *January 2018*

Rescue Alaska Mystery:

Finding Justice

A Tess and Tilly Mystery:

The Christmas Letter

Road to Christmas Romance:
Road to Christmas Past

USA Today best-selling author Kathi Daley lives in beautiful Lake Tahoe with her husband Ken. When she isn't writing, she likes spending time hiking the miles of desolate trails surrounding her home. She has authored more than seventy-five books in eight series, including Zoe Donovan Cozy Mysteries, Whales and Tails Island Mysteries, Sand and Sea Hawaiian Mysteries, Tj Jensen Paradise Lake Series, Writers' Retreat Southern Seashore Mysteries, Rescue Alaska Paranormal Mysteries, and Seacliff High Teen Mysteries. Find out more about her books at **www.kathidaley.com**

Stay up to date:
Newsletter, *The Daley Weekly*
http://eepurl.com/NRPDf
Kathi Daley Blog – publishes each Friday
http://kathidaleyblog.com
Webpage – **www.kathidaley.com**
Facebook at Kathi Daley Books –
www.facebook.com/kathidaleybooks
Kathi Daley Books Group Page –
https://www.facebook.com/groups/569578823146850/
E-mail – **kathidaley@kathidaley.com**
Twitter at Kathi Daley@kathidaley –
https://twitter.com/kathidaley
Amazon Author Page –
https://www.amazon.com/author/kathidaley
BookBub –
https://www.bookbub.com/authors/kathi-daley
Pinterest – **http://www.pinterest.com/kathidaley/**